C000018236

BETTING ON LOVE

Ann Patrick

A KISMET° Romance

METEOR PUBLISHING CORPORATION
Bensalem, Pennsylvania

KISMET® is a registered trademark of Meteor Publishing Corporation

Copyright © 1993 Patricia A. Kay
Cover Art Copyright © 1993 Alan Reingold

All rights reserved.

No part of this book may be reproduced, stored in a retrieval system, or transmitted in any form, by any means, including mechanical, electronic, photocopying, recording or otherwise, without prior written permission of the publisher, Meteor Publishing Corporation, 3369 Progress Drive, Bensalem, PA 19020.

First Printing August 1993.

ISBN: 1-56597-081-0

All the characters in this book are fictitious. Any resemblance to actual persons, living or dead, is purely coincidental.

Printed in the United States of America.

To Janis Robinson, a wonderful friend who left us at a far too young age, and her daughters, Kathy, Carol, and Laurie, who will always keep her memory alive.

ANN PATRICK

Ann Patrick has had a lifelong love affair with books. Other loves include her grandchildren, shopping, collecting elephants and watches, movies, Broadway shows, Calvin & Hobbes, music, the company of family and friends, traveling, animals, Cajun food, and getting mail. Ann lives with her husband and two cats in Houston, Texas, and she loves to hear from readers. You can write Ann at P.O. Box 441603, Houston, TX 77244-1603.

Other books by Ann Patrick:

PROLOGUE

August—New York City

Michael Vellini stared at his father. "I wish you'd reconsider," he said slowly.

Victor returned his stare, dark eyes enigmatic behind his bifocals. "Why?"

Michael hesitated a moment, knowing his father wasn't going to like what he planned to say. "Look, Dad, going into a company and studying their books is one thing. Spying on employees to catch a crook is a completely different matter."

Victori Vellini tented his hands. "Are you saying you think I should just forget about the fact that someone's been stealing from the casino?"

"No, of course not." Agitated now, Michael paced over to the big corner window overlooking Fifth Avenue. Far below he saw dozens of yellow cabs jostling for position on the wide thoroughfare. He could almost hear the blare of their horns as they honked at pedestrians, who, in typical New Yorker fashion, ignored them.

In the distance Michael could see a gleaming jet banking in preparation to land at LaGuardia. He sighed, turning to face his father, who had swiveled his chair around in Michael's direction. "But what I *am* saying is that you should forget this cloak-and-dagger stuff. Turn the whole mess over to the cops and let them take care of it."

"No police." Victor's dark eyes, hard and unrelenting, looked like shiny black marbles in his tanned face.

Count to ten, Michael told himself, knowing that losing his temper would never work. The more Michael or anyone opposed him, the more Victor would dig in his heels.

Victor Vellini was a determined, single-minded man when it came to his businesses. Hell, when it came to anything. And he'd never lost that old-world Italian mentality handed down from his parents—a mentality that said, when we have trouble, we take care of it in our own way, with our own kind.

Michael shrugged. "Okay. No police. But there *are* agencies who specialize in this kind of thing. *Professionals.*" In other words, people who know what they're doing. His gaze met his father's, willing him to be reasonable. "Let's hire one of them."

"Michael, I don't know why you're so squeamish all of a sudden. It isn't like you haven't ever gone into one of my companies when there's been a problem."

"I know that," Michael said patiently, "but that's different. All those other times I've gone in as myself. Everyone knew, up front, that I was your son. This seems dishonest."

"Dishonest! *We're* not the ones stealing from the

casino. How is it dishonest to try to catch someone who's taking what belongs to us?''

Michael shrugged. "Let's put it this way. I don't want to do it.''

"Are you refusing to do what I've asked?'' Now Victor's voice was as hard as his eyes.

"I'm asking you nicely to let me off the hook.''

"And if I say no?''

Michael sighed in frustration. "Then maybe I'll just have to say no, too.'' Michael could be every bit as stubborn as his father. He'd learned from a master.

"Have you forgotten that you work for me?''

Michael suppressed a smile. "How could I forget? You remind me of it at least twice a week.''

"I shouldn't have to remind you, Michael.'' Victor's voice sounded pained.

Michael threw up his hands. "I know, I know. I've heard it all so many times, I could repeat it in my sleep. All these years you've worked your tail off to leave something behind for your children. I should be grateful, willing to do anything my father asks. If I were a *loyal* son, I'd—''

"It's a sad day when a son shows such disrespect to his father,'' Victor said, interrupting Michael's exasperated speech. "In the old days, no son would ever speak to his father in such a way.'' Victor shook his head sadly. "My father would turn over in his grave if he could hear you.''

"All we need now are violins,'' Michael muttered under his breath. *Don't lose your temper. Count to twenty, take a deep breath, and answer him calmly.*

Michael walked around to the front of his father's desk, and sank into one of the two Italian leather chairs. He crossed his long legs and studied his father. Victor didn't look his sixty-nine years. Any stranger seeing him on the street would think he was in his late fifties, at most. He was tanned and fit, his thick hair still retaining its dark brown color. A man of average height, he was compactly built, with the physique of a laborer, although Victor's labors had been intellectual rather than physical.

Michael admired and respected his father for what he had accomplished. From humble beginnings he'd become a millionaire several times over.

Everyone said Victor Vellini had the Midas touch, both professionally and personally. But a few short years ago his luck changed. His beloved wife, Rosalie, had been diagnosed with breast cancer. The diagnosis came too late to save her. Six months later she was dead.

Victor had been heartbroken.

Unfortunately, Rosalie's death came just as Michael had made a decision. He wanted out. From the day he'd graduated from the Wharton School of Business, Michael had worked for his father. His role had gradually evolved to that of a troubleshooter. When Victor, who made a habit of buying businesses in trouble, acquired a company, Michael went in, did a thorough investigation, and gradually uncovered the problems. Then the problems were fixed.

And that usually meant heads rolled. People were fired. Lives were turned upside down.

For years Michael told himself it was part of the job. He told himself it wasn't his fault these people had made such stupid decisions. He told himself it was a dog-eat-dog world out there, that if you couldn't handle the heat, you shouldn't be in the kitchen.

But nothing he told himself made him feel any better about what he did.

He was a hatchet man.

He hated being a hatchet man.

From the time he'd worked as a waiter to earn his own spending money while in college, Michael had loved the restaurant business.

For years he'd saved part of his generous salary with the goal of starting his own restaurant someday. And right before his mother died, he'd been planning to tell his father he was leaving Vellini, Incorporated.

Gently, of course.

But then Rosalie died.

And Victor was devastated.

And Michael couldn't add to his devastation. He knew he'd have to wait awhile longer, so he put his plans and dreams on hold.

Now here he was, three years later, still doing hatchet jobs. Still trying to be the perfect son. He sighed deeply. "Dad, you know I love and respect you. . . ."

Victor said nothing.

"For nine years I've done everything you've asked of me. No matter how I felt about the jobs I was sent to do, I did them. But I'm tired—"

"You're tired! What do *you* have to be tired about? *I'm* the one who slaved to build the Vellini fortunes, and *you're* the one who's going to benefit, you and and your sister!" Victor's face was red by the time he finished.

Michael stared at Victor. "Are you finished?" he said softly.

Father and son locked gazes. Michael refused to be the first one to look away. Finally Victor, in a rare instance of capitulation, said, "What is this nonsense, you're tired? Tired of what?"

Michael knew Victor well enough to know that he always tried intimidation first. Since it hadn't worked, he had moved into his show-him-how-reasonable-I-can-be mode. "It isn't nonsense. I'm tired of what I do. You know that. You've just refused to face it. I'm not you. I don't like my job, and I want out."

"Michael, my son, you're talking foolishness."

Michael uncrossed his legs. He sat up straighter. "Stop that. I'm thirty-two years old. A grown man. I know my own mind, and I'm telling you, I don't like what I do, and I no longer want to do it."

"How can you say you don't like what you do?" Victor gestured at the lavish office. "All this will be yours someday. Whether you like it or not, you must be prepared to take over. I won't live forever, you know." He gave Michael a calculating look. "Your mother didn't," he added softly.

Michael couldn't sit a moment longer. He stood, jammed his hands into his pockets. "That was a low blow."

"I'm sorry if you think so, Michael, but nevertheless, it's the truth. I *won't* live forever."

"Quit trying to lay that guilt trip on me. It's not going to work this time."

"Michael, Michael, you disappoint me. You act as if I'm manipulating you."

Michael smiled cynically. "Aren't you?"

The two men stared at each other.

An Italian standoff, Michael thought. If this hadn't been such a serious subject, he might have been amused.

"Look . . ." he finally said. "I'll tell you what I'm

willing to do. I'll compromise. I'll go out to Vegas and infiltrate the employees at The Glass Slipper. I'll try to find out who's been stealing from the casino.''

Victor smiled triumphantly. "I knew—"

"But," Michael interrupted, "in return, we'll dispense with the games. You'll agree that this will be my last job for Vellini, Incorporated. When I've solved your problem at the casino, you won't give me any more guff about striking out on my own.''

Victor's smile faded. "To do what?"

"To open my own restaurant.''

The office became very quiet. Long seconds later, Victor sighed heavily. "I thought you'd forgotten that ridiculous notion by now.''

"I've never forgotten it, and it's not ridiculous.''

"Why would you want to open a restaurant when you—''

"I've given you all my reasons before.''

"Your reasons don't make sense.''

"Maybe they don't make sense to you. But as I said before, I'm not you. You did what you wanted to do. At least allow me the same consideration.''

"Michael . . .''

"I've made up my mind this time. Nothing is going to change it.''

"All right, Michael," Victor said, a long-suffering look crossing his face. "You win. But only because I know this whim of yours won't last.''

Michael sighed.

"You're too intelligent to spend your days running a restaurant!" Victor insisted. "I predict that before a year is up, you'll be bored and ready for something different.'' He smiled confidently. "You'll be back.''

Don't be too sure of that, Michael thought.

Still smiling, Victor reached for his intercom. "Now I'm going to call Dominic in. We'd better get started on planning our strategy if we're going to catch our crook."

Ten minutes later, Michael and his father were joined by Dominic Cassione, Michael's godfather and Victor's right-hand man and friend of sixty-three years.

"So . . . it begins," Dominic said, smiling. He rubbed his hands together.

Michael grinned. His godfather loved a challenge.

"Michael," Victor said. "Perhaps you should fill us in on your research."

Michael opened his notebook. "Our primary suspect is Philip Brownlee, the head pit boss." He consulted his notes. "Brownlee's been at The Glass Slipper twenty-four years, and he's been the head pit boss for three years." He looked up, meeting first his father's, then Dominic's gaze. "And it was just about three years ago that the blackjack revenues began to fall."

"Could be a coincidence," Dominic said.

"I don't believe in coincidence," Michael countered.

"Go on," said Victor impatiently.

"The other suspects are the three pit bosses, the head cashier, and various floormen and dealers. None of these employees could be stealing on their own, though. Not with the safeguards that are in place. No, this is a team effort. The trick will be to identify the players."

They talked about casino procedures for a while, with Michael explaining what he'd learned.

"Where do you plan to begin your investigation?" Dominic asked.

"Well . . ." Michael rubbed his chin. "The best place to start seems to be with one of the dealers— Shawn MacInnes."

Dominic raised his eyebrows. "I though you said Brownlee—"

"I did, but Shawn MacInnes is Philip Brownlee's niece." Michael sighed. "Getting to know her looks like the quickest way to get close to Brownlee."

Victor nodded. "The weakest link . . ."

"Do you think she's involved, too?" Dominic asked.

"It's possible," Michael said, thinking it was a strong possibility.

They talked for another hour, deciding that Dominic would be named the new general manager of The Glass Slipper, and in the process of assuming management, he would order the hiring of additional personnel.

Michael would be one of those hired.

"We'll make sure you're assigned to the same shift as the MacInnes woman, of course," Dominic said. "After that, it'll be up to you."

"I really hate this," Michael said.

"This is business," Victor said coldly. "There's no place for feelings in business."

Michael nodded. He knew that.

He knew that all too well.

ONE

Early October—Las Vegas

The little baldheaded man was cheating. Shawn Mac-Innes frowned in concentration as she watched his pudgy hands. She was ninety-nine percent sure his bet at the beginning of the hand had been three dollars. Now she saw there were four silver dollar tokens on his betting circle.

Her glasses slid down her nose, and she pushed them up, her heart accelerating.

She wasn't frightened. She had caught other cheaters over her past seven years of working as a blackjack dealer. But tension stretched her nerves taut as she glanced around casually, trying to catch the eye of Luis Alvarado, her floorman. She didn't see him anywhere.

Reaching under her table, she pressed the silent alarm that would alert the pit boss to trouble. Then she deftly began paying off the players.

Seconds later she felt rather than saw the presence of Jimmy Penner, the pit boss this shift, behind her.

Shawn waited as the four players at her table placed their next bets. The little baldheaded man fingered his chips, then pushed two five-dollar chips into his circle. It was the highest bet he'd made that evening.

Shawn dealt the first two cards to each player, including herself. As she did, a piercing pain shot down her neck and into her right shoulder—an occupational hazard of dealing, and something that seemed to get worse the longer she worked at her job. Between that and the ever-present haze of smoke in the casino, which bothered her so much, she couldn't wear her contacts at work, Shawn often wondered if the money she made as a dealer was worth the discomfort she suffered.

Sighing, she turned to the first player on her left—a skinny, dark-haired woman who had chain-smoked since sitting at Shawn's table. The woman had a king of hearts showing. With a satisfied smile, she pushed her cards under her bet. She would stand pat.

The baldheaded man was next. Shawn waited patiently for him to decide whether he wanted another card.

Out of the corner of her eye, she could see Jimmy Penner pacing slowly a few feet away. Then he turned his back to the table, but she knew he was intently watching the mirrors.

A short-skirted cocktail waitress approached her table. Several of the players ordered drinks. During the small disruption the baldheaded man brushed the felt top of the table with the two cards he held.

Shawn pulled the top card from the shoe and slid it over in front of him. She flipped it over with a soft slap.

The four of hearts.

Raising her eyebrows in a silent question, she waited. The little man's shiny forehead creased in thought. His pale blue eyes glanced furtively around the table. He eyed her exposed card—the six of diamonds—then pursed his lips and fiddled with the stack of chips in front of him.

Shawn knew he was trying to draw her attention away from the hand holding the cards. She held her breath and pretended to look in the other direction. With lightning speed, the baldheaded man slipped his cards under his bet, and when he removed his hands, there were now three five-dollar chips on his betting circle instead of two.

Shawn stared at the chips, then slowly raised her eyes to his round face. Sweat beads stood out on his upper lip. He refused to meet her eyes. The thin woman sitting next to him cleared her throat. The noisy ragtime music in the background suddenly seemed louder, the rat-a-tat-tat of the snare drums an accompaniment to Shawn's inner tension.

Turning slightly, she said, "Mr. Penner. Would you come here, please?"

She saw Jimmy raise his left hand in a beckoning gesture, and Luis Alvarado, her floorman, and a tall, good-looking, dark-haired man she'd never seen before moved in unison toward her table. As they approached, Shawn's gaze met the unknown man's. Immediately something flickered in the depths of his golden-brown eyes, and Shawn shivered with an odd sense of déjà vu. Her anxiety increased as the two men came closer.

"What's the problem here?" asked Jimmy, who now stood directly behind her. The question broke the spell cast over Shawn by the disturbing presence of the newcomer.

"This gentleman is cheating," she said softly, her head slightly inclined toward the baldheaded man.

"What? What did you say?" the baldheaded man blustered. He stood suddenly, knocking his drink off the table in the process.

"He had two five-dollar chips placed, but when he slid his cards under his bet, he added another five-dollar chip," Shawn said, her calm voice belying the strain this kind of situation always produced.

"That's a lie!" he shouted.

Shawn raised her eyes and gave him a level, unwavering look. He stared back for a few seconds, then dropped his gaze.

"I'll never play in this dump again, that's for sure!" he said, his voice squeaking to a crescendo. "This place sucks! Is this the way you cheat your customers out of their winnings? Huh? Huh?"

Some perverse part of Shawn admired the little man's bravado even as she despised his cheating.

"Give the gentleman three five-dollar chips to cover his bet," said Jimmy. "Then Michael here will escort him over to the security guard."

Shawn's gaze flickered to that of the man named Michael. And once again she felt that odd sense of recognition, and wondered why. She had to give herself a mental shake and forcibly turn her attention back to her table.

Calmly she placed the three five-dollar chips in front of the cheater. He glared at her and the three men confronting him, his face red and furious-looking. He had a lot of nerve. She'd give him that.

Breathing hard, he grabbed the chips and muttered

defiantly, "I'll leave, but only 'cause I want to. Who wants to play in this sleazy place, anyways? You can't make me do anything I don't wanna do."

Michael said in a firm, low-pitched voice, "I'll just walk with you to the security guard, and he'll take you over to the cashier's cage to cash in your chips. Then you'll leave by the front door and you won't come back. Is that understood?"

Like air being let out of a balloon, all the fight left the little man. He sputtered once, but he allowed Michael to lead him away.

Shawn's knees suddenly felt weak and she stared at the back of Michael's dark head. The other players at her table all had wide eyes and whispered among themselves.

"Take a break," ordered Jimmy. "It's time anyway." He beckoned toward another dealer who had just entered the pit.

Shawn picked up her tokes—dealer slang for the tokens given as tips by players at their tables—and gratefully relinquished the table. "Thanks, guys." As she moved away from the table, she looked at Luis, who shrugged.

"I can't believe people try this kind of thing," he muttered. "They really think they can outsmart us. Jeez!"

Shawn nodded again. It had always amazed her that anyone believed the high-stakes world of Nevada gambling would be so carelessly run that amateur crooks could just walk into a casino and take money that didn't belong to them.

Shawn wondered if, like her father, the baldheaded man was a compulsive gambler who desperately needed to win—if that was what drove him.

The undimmed pain of old hurts threatened to overtake her as she threaded her way around the gaming tables, but she determinedly pushed thoughts of her father from her mind.

By the time she reached the dealers' lounge, she had regained her equanimity. She pushed the door to the lounge open and looked around slowly. There were several dozen people scattered throughout the smoke-filled room. Shawn knew most of them by sight, although in a casino as large as The Glass Slipper, personnel changes came too often to keep up with the enormous staff.

"Shawn! Over here!"

The voice belonged to Liz Forrest, one of Shawn's best friends and a former roommate. Shawn spied the tall brunette sitting with two other dealers at a table in the far corner of the room.

"I'll be right there," she called. She walked toward the soft drink machine. Fishing two quarters out of her pocket, she inserted them into the machine, punched the button for diet cola, and waited.

Nothing happened.

"Oh, rats!" she muttered. She jabbed at the button again. Still nothing. In frustration she kicked the machine.

"Hey," said a low voice. "Aren't you the same lady who was so cool under pressure just a few minutes ago?"

Shawn whirled around, embarrassment heating her face. Topaz eyes, filled with amusement, gazed down at her.

"I put two quarters in and nothing came out," she explained breathlessly, caught by that same odd feeling of recognition that had assailed her earlier.

"What was it you wanted? Maybe I can help."

"A diet cola." She shifted uncomfortably under his warm appraisal.

"That sounds easy enough," he said. He turned toward the machine, and Shawn had a chance to study him. She guessed him to be about six one or six two, because he was much taller than she was, and she stood five feet six in her stockinged feet.

He was narrow-hipped with a loose, athletic stance and long legs. His shoulders were nicely broad, and Shawn idly wondered if he worked out to look so fit. Although he wasn't movie star handsome, he was very attractive with thick, black hair, sharp eyes, and lean good looks.

His face was especially arresting, she thought, with its strong lines, bold nose, and deep tan.

He was also one of those men who oozed sex appeal and charm, the kind Shawn always avoided like she avoided the scorching Nevada sun.

The kind who were never interested in her, anyway.

As she watched, he tilted the machine. To her chagrin, a can of the soda fell with a loud thunk into the tray at the bottom of the machine.

"Madam," he said with a flourish. His sharply chiseled face broke into a lazy smile, revealing even, white teeth. He handed her the cold drink.

"Thanks," said Shawn. Still embarrassed by her earlier display of temper, she added, "I feel a bit silly about kicking the machine."

That smile of his was dangerous. Just as the thought formed, it hit her.

Her father.

Michael's smile, Michael himself, reminded her of

her father. No wonder she felt as if she already knew him.

The dangerous smile widened. "I've always heard redheads were hot-tempered." His gaze rested on her hair, then swept boldly down her body. "But I like fiery women, especially beautiful fiery women." His eyes sparkled with good humor.

If Shawn hadn't already decided this man was too much like her father for comfort, that statement about her being beautiful would have done it.

Shawn knew she wasn't beautiful, and only a man who felt it was his mission in life to conquer every woman in his path would ever say so. Oh, yes, she thought. Just like her father, who had routinely charmed the socks off every woman he'd ever met, including his daughter.

Like Gerald MacInnes, this man was probably accustomed to women falling all over him, ready to give him anything and everything his little old heart desired.

Well, she had learned a hard lesson seven years ago, a lesson she didn't intend to repeat. So Michael whatever-his-last-name-was could be as smooth and charming and wonderful as he wanted to be, but it wouldn't do him a bit of good as far as Shawn was concerned. She didn't intend to become one of his worshippers.

Shawn gave him her most withering look, the one she'd perfected in those agonizing months after her father's death. Ignoring his remark, she said, "My friends are waiting for me. Thanks for your help." She turned away, but he reached out and caught her arm.

Short of being rude and tugging her arm from his grasp, Shawn had no choice but to stop.

"Hey," he said softly, "don't go away mad."

Shawn sighed loudly. "I'm not mad. I'm thirsty."
Maybe he'd take the hint and leave her alone. But his
warm hand still gripped her lower arm, and through the
sleeve of her white satin blouse, she could feel the heat
of contact. A slight tremor passed through her body.

She looked over her shoulder. Now his smile was
sheepish and his topaz eyes were no longer mocking.
"I guess I came on too strong, didn't I?"

Even as she told herself he had perfected that little-
boy-caught-with-his-hand-in-the-cookie-jar expression,
that he used it to dissolve a woman's defenses and gain
her trust, Shawn could feel herself responding to it.

"I only have about ten minutes of my break left,"
she said evenly, willing herself to resist him. "And as
I said before, my friends are waiting for me." She
pushed her glasses up, avoiding his eyes.

"But I don't even know your name," he said reasonably. "After all, I rescued a damsel in distress, so the
least you can do is tell me your name. I'm Michael.
Michael . . . DeNiro."

Shawn looked up at him. The good humor was back
in his eyes. She wanted to tell him to take his hand off
her arm and go find someone else to dazzle. *Leave me
alone*, she thought frantically. What did he want with
her? All he had to do was look around him; there must
be dozens of other women in the casino who were
better-looking and more glamorous than she was. More
fun, too, she imagined.

She sighed again. Even if Michael DeNiro had been
her type, and he wasn't, she was no good at this. She'd
never learned the art of casual flirting. She always felt
awkward, stupid, and completely out of her depth. But
she knew it was churlish of her to refuse to tell him
her name.

She shrugged. "My name is Shawn MacInnes. *Now* can I go, please?"

He finally released her arm and extended his right hand. "Nice to meet you, Shawn MacInnes."

After hesitating only a moment, Shawn placed her smaller hand in his. The contact caused a tiny jolt of pleasure to shimmy through her.

She could have kicked herself. *What is the matter with you? Do you want him to know you're attracted to him? Do you want to encourage him?*

Stiffening her back, she tugged her hand away, saying, "Well, thanks again, Mr. . . . DeNiro, was it?"

"Michael," he said.

"Michael," she repeated. "Now if you'll excuse me . . ." Without a backward glance, she marched briskly away. She could feel his eyes watching her.

As she dropped into the vacant chair at Liz's table, Liz said, "Yum, yum. Who was *that*?"

Shawn shrugged and raised her can of soda to her lips. She took a long, refreshing swallow and said, "His name is Michael DeNiro. I think he's one of the new people training to be floormen, but that's just a guess. He and Luis and Jimmy helped me bounce a cheater earlier."

"What a hunk!" Liz said, her expressive face leering in admiration. She grinned as Shawn frowned. "Well, he *is*, Shawn. I can't believe you don't agree." The grin was accompanied by a devilish glint in her gray eyes as she said suggestively, "In fact, Michael DeNiro can park his shoes under my bed any old time he chooses!"

"Oh, for heaven's sake!" Shawn said before she could stop herself. "Is that all you ever think about?" She could feel herself blushing again, and it infuriated her. Why couldn't she be casual about sex and men the way Liz was? The way her roommate, Annika, was? The way every other woman over the age of fifteen seemed to be? Why did she have to give away her feelings so vividly?

The other two girls at their table giggled. "What else *is* there to think about?" one of them said.

"Yeah," the other said with a dramatic sigh. "I think about it all the time. . . ."

Liz grinned and winked at the other two. "You know, Shawn," she drawled, "there's something seriously wrong with you. A twenty-eight-year-old woman who doesn't think about sex isn't normal!"

Shawn opened her mouth to retort, then closed it again. What was the use? They'd had this discussion before. Every word Liz said was true. Well, almost every one. Shawn *did* think about sex. She thought about it a lot.

She simply didn't do it. And not because she didn't have the same desires and needs as other women, but because she was waiting for the right man to come along, and if she'd learned anything in twenty-eight years, it was that the right man wasn't going to be anything like Michael DeNiro.

Shawn had goals, one of which was to get as far away from Las Vegas and the gambling industry as she could. The other two were to save enough money to devote herself to her painting full time and to find a nice, sane, ordinary man—one who got up when the sun came up and went to bed when the sun went down.

Someone who didn't gamble.

Someone who wouldn't let her down as her father had let her and her mother down.

Someone who had goals in life that extended beyond the gratification of the moment.

Without exception, all the men she knew had one thing on their minds. To get a woman into bed. Period.

"Well, you may not be curious about Michael De-Niro, but I certainly am," Liz said.

"Knowing you, Liz, you'll know his entire life history by the end of the week," Shawn said.

Liz laughed and drained her can of root beer. "If I don't, it won't be for lack of trying; you can bet your boots on that." She gave Shawn an arch look. "Course, if you want him, sweetie, he's all yours. After all, you saw him first."

Shawn ignored the taunt and glanced up at the wall clock. "It's almost three-fifteen, Liz. We'd better get back to the tables."

Each blackjack dealer at The Glass Slipper worked an eight-hour shift, with a fifteen-minute break each hour. Shawn and Liz were currently working swing shift—eight P.M. to four A.M.—and they only had forty-five minutes left before they would be finished for the day.

As they walked together out of the lounge, Liz nudged Shawn. "You never answered me. Does that mean you want Michael—" she drawled his name "—for yourself?" She spoke loudly to be heard over the incessant noises of the casino: the clang of the slot machines, the blaring of the ragtime music, and the babble of excited voices.

Shawn shook her head. "I'm not the least bit interested in him, Liz. He's all yours."

TWO

Michael watched his quarry leave the lounge with her dark-haired friend. He rubbed his chin thoughtfully. So that was Shawn MacInnes.

She'd been a shock, he had to admit it. The woman was nothing like he'd expected.

He certainly had not expected to like her. In fact, he'd looked upon his mission to get to know Shawn, and through her, her uncle Philip, as one of the most unsavory aspects of this job, one he intended to conclude as quickly as possible.

In the six weeks since his meeting with his father, Michael had done his homework. He'd carefully studied and memorized the files on all the employees who were suspects, especially Shawn and her uncle.

He knew she was twenty-eight years old, that her father had been a compulsive gambler, and that he'd committed suicide.

He knew that Shawn had been an art student at the time of the suicide, that she'd been forced to drop out of school and work full time, that for the past seven years she'd worked as a blackjack dealer.

He knew Shawn and her mother, a dance teacher, had struggled for years to pay off Gerald MacInnes' debts. He also knew that a year ago, Shawn's uncle Philip had finished paying off the remainder of her father's debts. To the tune of forty thousand dollars.

But those were just facts. Words on a piece of paper. Reading about someone couldn't tell you everything. And Shawn was a perfect example.

From her file, Michael had imagined a knowing, experienced type. Someone liberal and flamboyant—like the artsy women he'd known in New York. A woman who knew the score.

He'd known that files were often wrong. They'd certainly been wrong where Shawn was concerned. They'd given no indication he'd find a woman who, unless she was a consummate actress, seemed completely out of place in a city like Las Vegas.

Michael's first thought, when he'd gazed into Shawn's soft blue eyes and seen how disconcerted she was by his blatant flirting, was that she was an innocent. An untouched, gentle-spirited innocent. A lamb in a world of wolves. The kind of woman who belonged in an *Ozzie and Harriet* household instead of a casino.

He shook himself. Thoughts like those were dangerous. More than anyone else, Michael should know that.

Because no matter how Shawn MacInnes looked on the surface, there was no telling what she was like underneath. Until he got to know her, he could not afford to make a snap judgment.

He had to remember what his mission was. He was in Las Vegas to catch a crook. And that entailed finding out all he could about the management of The Glass Slipper.

Which meant he had to get close to Shawn MacInnes and her uncle as well as anyone else who might be helping themselves to some of the profits from blackjack.

Now, though, after meeting her and talking with her, Michael couldn't imagine a more unlikely candidate for larceny than Shawn. Still, a person never knew. Appearances could be deceiving. Some of the most violent criminals had innocent baby faces.

Sighing, wishing for the dozenth time this job were over, wishing he never had to wield another hatchet, wishing he could call up his father and tell him to take his job and stuff it, Michael lifted his can of cola, swallowed the last few drops, then took aim.

The empty can hit the wastebasket dead center. "Haven't lost my touch," he said to no one in particular. "Now let's hope I haven't lost my touch as the hatchet man, either."

Ten minutes later, Michael stood a few yards away from Shawn's table and watched her graceful movements as she worked. He told himself to be completely analytical. To study her, figure out what made her tick, and decide which approach to use in his campaign to win her confidence.

But no matter what he told himself, he couldn't seem to keep his mind focused. The problem was, he thought wryly, Shawn MacInnes was just too damned appealing.

Even those granny glasses, which should have detracted from her appeal, enhanced it in his eyes. They made her look defenseless and vulnerable.

As he watched, she bent her head. Under the bright casino lights and mirrors, the red-gold of her thick, curly hair gleamed like newly polished copper. Although she'd tried to confine it with a large gold barrette, it was a losing battle. Wild tendrils curled in haphazard fashion around her face and neck. Little Orphan Annie hair, he thought, and that, too, added to her aura of youth and innocence.

Michael especially liked the smattering of freckles dotted over Shawn's nose and the sprinkling that filled the vee-neck of her blouse. There was something about freckles on a woman's chest . . .

He took a deep breath. *Come on, Vellini, keep your mind on the matter at hand. Figure out how you're going to win her friendship, not how much you like her freckles.*

Even his brief encounter with Shawn in the employees' lounge told him that winning her friendship wouldn't be easy.

"So you like her, huh?" said Luis Alvarado, who had walked up next to Michael.

Michael looked down at the shorter man. "What's not to like?"

Luis rubbed his chin. "Listen, man, if I were you, I'd forget all about that one."

"Oh? Why? She taken or something?"

"No, she's not taken, at least, not that I know of. But tryin' to get to first base with Shawn will just be a waste of time. Believe me, man. Lots of us have already tried." He shook his head. "Hell, I don't know what her problem is, but she don't have nothin' to do with any of us here at the casino."

Michael nodded, his gaze traveling back to Shawn. "Maybe I'll have better luck," he said softly. It wouldn't hurt to plant the idea in Luis' mind that Michael planned to try to get to know Shawn.

"Okay," Luis said. "If you wanna waste your time, it's no skin off my nose. But don't say I didn't warn you." He laughed. "Actually, it's gonna be fun to watch her knock you down!" Still laughing, he wandered off.

So Shawn had a reputation for being hard to get. That didn't surprise Michael. Not after her reaction to him in the employees' lounge. Well, he'd had tough nuts to crack before. From experience, he knew everyone had weak spots. He would simply have to find Shawn's. The thought gave him no pleasure. Thank God this was his last job.

Michael looked at his watch, a no-nonsense sports watch he preferred over the Rolex his father had given him the previous Christmas.

It was almost four o'clock. His shift would be over at four, and he guessed Shawn's would be, too. He was sure she'd already been working at midnight, so he didn't think she was on the night shift.

He wondered if she drove to work alone or if she was car-pooling. He decided he'd try to walk out with her.

Shawn went straight to the locker room, and since Michael hadn't stored anything in his locker, he didn't follow her in. He just waited outside. A few minutes later she emerged with a tan leather shoulder bag slung over her left arm. Right behind her was the dark-haired woman she'd spent her break with.

Shawn noticed him immediately, and before her delicate features tightened in annoyance, he thought he detected a flash of interest—maybe even pleasure—in those soft blue eyes. Quickly masked, but there for just an instant.

"Hi again," he said.

"Hello."

Her tone was cool. It clearly said, *Go away*.

Michael smiled at the dark-haired woman who was eyeing him with interest. "I don't think we've met," he said. "I'm Michael DeNiro."

"Liz Forrest." She grinned and stuck out her hand.

"Are you gals on your way out?" he asked.

Shawn's expression told him how much she thought of his stupid question. "Yes," she said with a resigned sigh. "We're on our way out."

"Do you mind if I walk out with you?" Perversely, even though he knew Shawn's keep-your-distance attitude toward him was going to make his job tougher, he admired the fact that she was aloof. That she hadn't given Luis Alvarado or the others he'd referred to the time of day. That she wasn't swayed by a good line.

"Would it matter if we did?" she said.

"Shawn!" Liz said. She gave Michael an arch look. "*I* don't mind if you walk out with us."

Ignoring him and her friend, Shawn strode off toward the back entrance. If Michael hadn't seen that revealing glint of pleasure when she'd first seen him standing outside the locker room, he might have been fooled by the rigid look of her back, the stiffness of her shoulders, and the jut of her chin.

But he *had* seen that glimmer she'd quickly hidden.

Liz gave him an apologetic shrug, and they fell in behind Shawn.

She stopped briefly to sign out with the security guard.

"Night, Shawn," the guard said.

"Goodnight, Benny." She glanced back. "I'll see you there, Liz."

"Okay," Liz said.

Shawn completely ignored Michael, who leaned over the sign-out book and hurriedly scribbled his name.

She took off toward the door, and Michael leaped ahead to push open the heavy metal exit door. She brushed past him without meeting his gaze, and they emerged into the employee parking lot.

It was October, a beautiful month in the desert. The sky was clear and studded with thousands of stars. If only the Las Vegas power brokers had been able to capture the brilliance and beauty of the stars in their endless quest for flash and spectacle, Michael thought, the Strip might look like a regal princess instead of a brazen lady of the night.

Without a backward glance, Shawn marched off.

Michael sprinted to catch her. "Shawn, stop."

She did. But she didn't turn around. "What do you want, Mr. DeNiro?"

"Michael." He touched her arm. Briefly.

She stiffened at his touch, but when he dropped his hand, she slowly turned, raising her eyes to meet his gaze. They were standing under a tall lamp, and its golden glow bathed her skin and shining hair.

She pushed up her glasses, an unconscious gesture he'd noticed earlier. "Michael," she said softly. "What do you want from me?"

Michael knew whatever he said now would make a big difference in how their relationship progressed. "Look, I'm not going to attack you. I'm not going to force myself on you. I just . . . well, I'm new in Vegas," he said sincerely, because he *was* new there, that was no lie. "I don't have any friends here. I just thought maybe you and I could be friends."

Silence. Then slowly, "Why me?"

Michael pressed his advantage. "I like you."

"You don't even know me."

"That's the point. I want to get to know you."

"I—"

"Come on, Shawn. Take pity on a lonesome guy. How about if we just go have a cup of coffee somewhere? Coffee and conversation. That's it . . . I promise."

She shook her head. "No, I can't."

"Can't? Or won't?"

She eyed him thoughtfully. When she spoke, her voice was firm, and Michael thought he could hear a faint twinge of regret, but maybe that was wishful thinking on his part.

"Look, Michael," she said slowly. "I'm already meeting someone this morning. But even if I wasn't, I wouldn't go with you. Now, I don't want to hurt your feelings. I'm sure you're a really nice guy. I'm also sure you could go back inside and ask any one of a dozen women to go have coffee with you, and they'd probably all jump at the chance. So why don't you?" And then she turned and walked away.

Thoughtfully Michael watched her.

Someone cleared a throat behind him.

Michael turned. Liz stood a few feet away. She studied him for a moment, then grinned. "I was supposed to meet Shawn for breakfast at Denny's. Would you like to go in my place?"

All the way to Denny's, Michael whistled.

Shawn drove slowly up Las Vegas Boulevard, commonly referred to as the Strip by natives and tourists alike. She paid scant attention to the people walking on the sidewalks or the other cars on the street. Even when some hotshot in a white Corvette whipped around to pass her, she barely blinked. She was too preoccupied with thoughts of Michael DeNiro.

What did he want with her?

And why had it been so hard to say no to him?

You know why. He made your toes curl.

Shawn squirmed uncomfortably. She had this irritating habit of not being able to lie to herself.

Well, she thought, it didn't matter if he made her toes curl or not. She was absolutely, positively *not* going to succumb to his wiles.

Ten minutes later, she pulled into the Denny's parking lot. The first thing she saw was Michael, long legs crossed in front of him, leaning casually against a white Corvette.

Her heart went *boing*.

What in the world is he doing here? she thought. He was obviously waiting for her. But how . . . ?

Liz.

Of course.

Shawn decided she would strangle Liz the minute she got her alone.

Yet as irritated as she was by Liz's sneakiness, Shawn couldn't help feeling a stirring of excitement. She could tell herself a million times that Michael DeNiro wasn't her type, that she wasn't interested in him, and that she wanted him to leave her alone. But the fact remained that she was drawn to him.

You'd better be darned careful, Shawn. This man could mean trouble.

She looked at him standing there, the very picture of male conceit as he leaned against his car. Honestly! A

Corvette! Of all the clichés. Actually, though, she wasn't surprised. If she'd thought about the kind of car a man like Michael would drive, she would have expected it to be a car like this one. Hadn't her father driven a low-slung, fast sports car?

Shawn parked her eight-year-old Honda Civic, and by the time she'd turned off the ignition, picked up her purse from the passenger seat, and taken a deep breath to fortify herself, Michael was already opening her car door.

When he reached for her hand to help her out, their eyes met, and he smiled—that slow, lazy smile that had probably worked its magic on untold numbers of women.

But even knowing this, even knowing she was an absolute fool to let his smile affect her, something inside Shawn's chest tightened, and for a moment her breath caught. And yes, her stupid toes curled.

"Surprised to see me here?" he said.

"Not really. Liz invited you, didn't she?"

"Yep." His hand settled in the small of her back, guiding her across the parking lot.

She tried to ignore the pleasant tingle where his warm palm connected with her body.

"You're not mad, are you?" he asked.

"Why should I be mad?" She looked up, meeting his warm golden gaze. "After all, you're *Liz's* guest."

His eyes twinkled as he leaned over and whispered in her ear. "Liz isn't the reason I came. You are."

Oh, he was smooth. He probably thought she was taken in by his melting brown eyes. . . .

Quit thinking about his eyes!

Shawn hurriedly dropped her gaze.

They walked into the restaurant, and Shawn looked

around for Liz. She didn't see her anywhere. The hostess walked up to them. "Two?" she said.

"No, there will be three of us," Shawn said. "Someone will be meeting us."

"We might as well get a booth," Michael suggested.

"But Liz—"

"This place is small. She'll see us."

The hostess led them to a street-side booth. To avoid looking at Michael, Shawn looked outside. Across the wide street—which, even at this time of night, still had both automobile and pedestrian traffic—the pink and white neon lights of The Flamingo flashed garishly.

"Are you hungry?" Michael asked, handing her a menu.

"Actually, I'm starving." Shawn accepted the menu, then tapped her finger impatiently against the tile tabletop. "Where *is* she?"

Michael shrugged. "Maybe she changed her mind."

"She wouldn't *do* that," Shawn said through gritted teeth. But suddenly she knew Liz would. Shawn decided strangling was too humanitarian. She would instead give Liz a slow-working, very painful poison.

Their waitress, an ordinary-looking, middle-aged blonde, materialized at their table, and she stood, pencil poised over her order pad. She looked at Shawn, raising her eyebrows questioningly.

"I guess I'll have the pancakes . . . with bacon. And a glass of milk." Shawn said, sighing and laying down her menu. What the heck. She was here. It would be very childish to get up and walk out.

The waitress looked at Michael. "And *you*, sir?"

"I'll have two scrambled eggs with sausage and an order of biscuits and gravy. And coffee." Michael gave the waitress the benefit of his winning smile. "On second thought, make that double sausage." He grinned at Shawn. "I'm starving, too." He handed his menu to the waitress, who almost, but not quite, batted her eyelashes at him. Giving him one more flirty look, the waitress left.

"How long does it take to get used to working these odd hours?" he asked. "I can't seem to get my mealtimes straightened out."

Still half-amused, half-irritated by what she'd just witnessed, but nonetheless relieved to have a safe topic of conversation, Shawn said, "It takes me a couple of days every time I switch from one shift to another."

"How often do you switch?"

"Didn't you get a schedule when you started work?" she asked.

He gave her a sheepish look. "Yes, but I didn't read it."

Shawn laughed. "We're on a nine-day rotation. Nine days of days, then three days off. Nine days of afternoons, then three days off. And so on, through swing shift and nights."

"Which shift do you like best?"

"Me? I like swing shift best."

"Why do you like swing shift best?"

"Better tips. More high rollers play during the hours of eight to four."

"But don't you hate giving up your entire evening?" He looked pointedly at her left hand, which was ringless. "You're single. Doesn't working the swing shift cramp your social life?"

Shawn almost said, *I don't have a social life*, and just caught herself in time. She shrugged, saying, "Most of my friends work in the casinos, too, so they understand."

He nodded, but his eyes glinted with something—something that said he knew she wasn't telling him the whole truth—but maybe that was just her own paranoia about her woeful lack of anything that passed for a social life.

"Well, at least you've got your days off," he said.

Shawn shifted uncomfortably. She wished he'd quit looking at her like that. "Well, yes . . ."

"You *do* have days off, don't you?"

"Yes, but . . ."

"But what?"

"Well, whenever I get the chance, I work my days off." But even as she silently berated herself, Shawn knew why she was volunteering information she didn't normally volunteer. It was because Michael seemed genuinely interested. Because he listened carefully, giving her his complete attention. His gaze didn't wander, and he didn't fidget.

He was either one of those rare individuals who really cared what other people thought and did, or he was the most practiced con artist she'd ever met.

Just then the waitress appeared with their food, and for the next few minutes they didn't talk. Finally, though, after both were about halfway through with their meal, Michael said, "It's none of my business, of course, but I can't help but wonder why you work so hard. Don't you know what they say about all work and no play?"

Shawn took a swallow of the milk she'd ordered. She debated telling him that it *was* none of his business why she worked so hard. But she knew he didn't deserve that kind of reaction to his question, which was perfectly legitimate. In fact, if she weren't so unwisely attracted to him, she wouldn't have thought a thing of it.

"I'm an artist," she finally said. "And I'm saving my money so that I can take a year off and paint."

"An artist, huh? What kind of painting do you do?"

"I mostly paint people. Not portraits. Just people doing things."

"Are you good?"

"I'm very good," she said, amazing herself—not only because she'd said something so out of character, but because she'd said it to him.

"I'll bet you are," he said softly, "But when do you find time to paint if you're always working?"

"I don't work *all* the time. Besides, I paint for a couple of hours every day before I go to work."

"I'd like to see your work."

Shawn's guard immediately went up. "Are you interested in art?"

"A little."

Shawn knew she was going to have to get over it, but she didn't show her work to just anyone. In fact, it was only recently she'd felt confident enough of her skill to hang several paintings on the walls of the town home she shared with Annika.

He returned to his meal and didn't pursue the subject. A few minutes later, he looked up and said, "This town is really incredible."

Shawn blinked. What was he talking about?

"Look at those two. . . ." He inclined his head toward two middle-aged women who had just been seated across from them. Both had paper tubs—the kind found next to all the slot machines in Vegas—full of silver. "They look like they should spend their evenings at the sewing circle meeting in the kind of town that rolls up the sidewalks at ten o'clock. Instead they're sitting in a restaurant in Las Vegas at—'' he looked at his watch ''—four forty-five in the morning . . . with their gambling loot on the table beside them.'' He frowned thoughtfully. ''What is it about gambling that attracts so many different kinds of people?''

Shawn studied him. Maybe he *wasn't* like her father. ''Don't *you* ever gamble?''

He smiled. ''Sometimes. But not this kind of gambling. I save mine for things I have a chance of winning.''

Something about his gaze gave Shawn that shivery feeling again. She knew he was flirting with her, telling her with his admiring look that he liked her. She wished she could think of some kind of clever retort, but her mind was a blank. Then she was saved from replying, because their waitress walked up to their table.

''You all right here?'' she asked. She began to remove their empty plates.

''Can I get more coffee?'' Michael asked, flashing her another smile.

The waitress smiled back, and Shawn could almost see her feathers fluffing.

See? she told herself. It's just a reflex. Men like him turn on the charm for anything in skirts, so don't get any ideas that he thinks you're special or anything.

Now it was Shawn's turn to look at her watch. It was almost five o'clock. ''Listen, you go ahead and drink your second cup of coffee,'' she said, ''but I've really got to be going.'' She lifted her purse from the seat and prepared to slide out of the booth.

''No, wait . . . Shawn, don't leave.'' He called to their waitress, who promptly came back. ''I changed my mind about the coffee. Can I just have our check?''

Shawn knew it would be rude to leave without waiting for him to pay the bill.

But she wanted to. Oh, how she wanted to.

Nameless fears churned in her stomach as, trapped by her own courteous upbringing, she waited.

Quit being such a coward. It's just a few more minutes, that's all. Then you can say good-bye and get away from him.

When the check came, she preceded him up the aisle. And after he'd paid the cashier, they walked out into the clear night together. Car horns and a blast of music from a nearby casino greeted them. Las Vegas, the city without clocks, ran twenty-four hours a day.

Shawn crossed the parking lot to her Honda. She turned to face Michael. "Thanks for breakfast," she said firmly, half turned away from him, already reaching for her car door.

"Shawn . . . wait a minute." He touched her shoulder.

Very slowly, she looked up.

"I've enjoyed this," he said softly, "and I'd really like to see you again."

It was very bright in the parking lot, and as Shawn met his warm gaze, something knotted way down in her belly. She took a deep breath. "I don't think so, Michael."

"I don't understand." He sounded honestly bewildered.

"Michael—"

"I thought you liked me."

"I *do* like you." Oh, darn it. This was exactly the situation she'd wanted to avoid. Why had she let herself get into this discussion? Why hadn't she just left the restaurant when she'd wanted to?

"Then what's the problem?"

"I just don't think it's a good idea for us to see each other again."

"Why not? I'm single. You're single. We like each other. Why *isn't* it a good idea for us to see each other?"

Shawn looked away, across the wide street. She tried to think of the best way to say what she knew needed saying. After a long moment she met his gaze squarely. "Listen, Michael. There's nothing personal in this. You're just not my type, all right? And since you're not, there'd be absolutely no point to going out with you. It would be a waste of my time and yours." She forced herself to smile, forced herself to push the regret for what could never be far away, forced herself to open her car door and slide in.

"Hey, wait a minute! You can't just say something like that and then leave."

"Michael, please . . ." Why didn't he just accept it? Why was he pushing her so?

"What do you mean, I'm not your type?"

Shawn sighed wearily. She looked up. "Okay. You asked for it. So I'll tell you. I have no intention of becoming involved with anyone like . . . with anyone who works in the gambling industry. Not now. Not ever. I've had all I can take of this kind of life-style. As soon as I have enough money—and hopefully that'll be this coming summer—I'm out of here. I'm going east, somewhere like Maine or Vermont, and I'm staying there. *Now* do you understand?" She inserted her key in the ignition. "Good night, Michael. I'm sure I'll be seeing you around." Then she shut the door and locked it, started the ignition, and drove out of the parking lot.

She didn't look back.

THREE

Michael stared after her car.

Well, I'll be damned, he thought. Wasn't this a frustrating development? Because he was pretending to be something he wasn't, Shawn wasn't interested in him.

Hey, buddy, if she knew who you really were and what you're really doing in Vegas, she'd be even less interested!

In fact, if she knew who Michael really was and what he was really doing in Las Vegas, she'd be justifiably angry at his attempts to get close to her.

Folding himself into his car, he pondered his problem. He continued to think about it while he drove to the small motel near the outskirts of town where he'd set up temporary quarters until he moved into his rented town home on Thursday.

Forget about Shawn. Something is telling her to stay away from you. Respect that. Leave her alone.

Michael sighed deeply. As much as he might want

to listen to his conscience, he couldn't. Because his first loyalty was to his father.

So what should he do?

Maybe he could tell her *part* of the truth. The part about his plans for opening his own restaurant. Maybe if she knew he had the same kinds of goals she did, she would be more receptive to him.

Even though her refusal to respond to his overtures had thrown a monkey wrench into his plans, Michael couldn't help admiring Shawn. That delicate exterior of hers was misleading. Underneath that sweet innocence beat the heart of a strong, determined woman.

Well, he had to be just as determined. Because the sooner he got this job over with, the sooner he could get on with his life.

As he parked his car, Michael wondered what Shawn would say when she discovered who her newest neighbor was.

Shawn woke up at eleven o'clock on Tuesday. Outside her bedroom window she heard a bird singing. She lay very still, listening. Some kind of warbler, she thought. Maybe an orange-crested one, if the weak trilling was any indication.

She'd always loved birds. When she was little, her father used to take her out on his days off. Armed with an Audubon guide and field glasses, they'd watch all the different species common to the West, and he would tell her about them. Before long, she had been able to identify some of the birds without any coaching from him.

She smiled, remembering those happy days before her entire world had crashed down around her. Before she had realized her father was a very different kind of man than she'd imagined him to be.

The sun, already full and strong, streamed through the partially opened slats of her miniblinds. She stretched and rubbed her grainy eyes. Waking in the middle of the day was the worst part about working swing shift.

Shawn had always loved early morning. She functioned best in early morning.

Soon, she promised herself. Soon you'll sleep at night and paint all day.

After her regular start-up ritual of coffee, a forty-minute run, a shower, and breakfast, she poured herself a second cup of coffee and headed back upstairs to the loft that had been justification enough to spend the extra money to rent this town home instead of a cheaper apartment. She wanted to get in at least two hours of painting today.

As she passed her roommate's bedroom, the door opened, and a sleepy-eyed Annika Carlsen yawned and said, "Hey . . . what time is it?"

Shawn grinned. "Noon."

Annika was a dancer. She danced with a big review at one of the larger hotels. And although she was usually finished working before midnight, she was a night owl, and if she didn't have a party to go to, or wasn't spending the night with her boyfriend, she'd come home and watch cable TV until the wee hours.

Annika yawned again and shuffled off toward the bathroom. Shawn continued on to the loft. Once there, she sat at the drawing table under the skylight. She looked at her painting in progress—another water-color—this one a rendering of a photograph she'd taken months earlier of a young boy playing Frisbee with his dog. It was about half-done, and Shawn was pleased with it.

Unlike many painters who worked with watercolors, Shawn did not use hazy washes of pale pastels or muted colors. She worked with vivid primary colors and bold strokes.

She winced as she began to paint, stopping to rub her right shoulder. Her occupational hazard sometimes played havoc with her painting, but she usually forced herself to paint whether her shoulder hurt or not. She couldn't afford to neglect her art.

Thirty minutes later, engrossed in her work, she didn't hear Annika come into the room.

"Shawn, you've got Friday off, don't you?"

Shawn jumped. "Annika, don't sneak up on me when I'm working!" she said, half-serious, half-teasing.

"Sorry." Annika grinned and leaned against the doorframe.

She looked gorgeous today, thought Shawn, a tiny prick of envy piercing her heart. Unlike Shawn, who felt she always looked ordinary, Annika always looked gorgeous. A long-legged blonde, she had perfect porcelain skin and huge green eyes. "Well, *are* you off Friday?"

"Uh-huh. I was supposed to be off tomorrow through Friday, but I agreed to work for Becky tomorrow and Thursday. Why?"

"Darryl's giving a party Friday night. He wants me to bring you." Darryl Anderson, a local real estate magnate, was Annika's current boyfriend.

Shawn started to shake her head. She hated parties.

"Now, don't say no. Darryl's cousin is in town, and he thinks you'd like him."

"Oh, no! I *hate* being fixed up, and you know it," Shawn protested.

"This isn't like being fixed up. You'll be at the party. Tod'll be at the party. Lots of other people'll be at the party. What's the problem?"

"What's this Tod like?" Shawn asked skeptically.

"He's supposed to be tall and handsome. He's an accountant, he's divorced, and he lives in New Hampshire. That's why Darryl thought of you. He knows how you're planning to go live up there and freeze your butt off. God knows why . . ." Annika said, rolling her eyes.

Annika came from Minnesota, where her Swedish great-grandparents had settled many years before. She'd told Shawn once that she never wanted to live in a cold climate again. Shawn, on the other hand, had always lived in the desert. She hated the heat, the sameness, the constant glare of the sun.

Her dreams were filled with snow, and fireplaces, and ice skates, and thick sweaters. She couldn't imagine anything more wonderful than living in New England.

"I don't know, Annika. . . ."

"Come on . . ." Annika wheedled. "You never do anything except work and paint. You've gotta get out and meet some people once in awhile." She wagged her finger. "How else do you expect to meet Prince Charming?" She grinned. "You know what they say, don't you?"

"If you're going to give me that line about all work and no play—"

"Who, *moi*?" Annika mugged. "No, what I was going to say was you've gotta kiss a lot of frogs to find a prince."

Shawn rolled her eyes. "When I move—"

"When you move, you'll do exactly the same things you do now," Annika predicted. "I'm not going to take no for an answer, and neither is Darryl. Some of the other kids from the show'll be there, and I'll bet Darryl's asked some of the gang from The Slipper, too. It'll be fun."

Maybe Michael will be there.

The thought, unbidden and unwanted, popped into her mind. She shoved it away. Michael DeNiro was the last person she wanted to see, so what difference did it make whether he was at the party or not?

Shawn sighed. "I'll think about it."

"You're going," Annika declared, "and that's final."

On Friday, when Shawn woke up, the first thing she did was look outside. Another bright, sunny day.

Anxious to get her run over with so she could get started painting, she gulped down her coffee, then hurriedly brushed her teeth and dressed, then did her warm-up exercises.

For at least the dozenth time since Tuesday, she regretted telling Annika she'd to go Darryl's party tonight. If she didn't have that obligation staring her in the face, she could paint until midnight if she wanted to.

You were really stupid to agree to giving up a big part of your only day off this week. She sighed. Oh, well. What's done is done. And if she wasn't having any fun, she could always leave early.

Finally ready for her run, she grabbed her keys and mini can of Mace, and walked out of the bedroom. At almost the same moment, Annika emerged from the bathroom. She was enveloped in her long white terry cloth robe and had a white towel wrapped turban fashion around her head. She grinned.

"You're up early today," Shawn commented.

"Yeah, well, I'm going over to Darryl's to help him get ready for tonight."

Shawn nodded. "I'm going out to run." She started down the stairs.

"While you're out, you might want to check out our new neighbor," Annika said. She began to towel her hair dry.

Shawn paused. "They rent out that unit down the street?"

"Uh-huh. Yesterday some guy moved in. At least I think it's just one guy. I didn't see any women. Anyway, check it out and give me the scoop, okay? He looked great from a distance."

Shawn laughed. "Boy, you're nosy. What do you want me to do? Go knock on his door and ask him if he's single?"

"Why not? Inquiring minds want to know . . . That's my motto."

"Yeah, yours and sixty million other people's . . ." Still chuckling, Shawn let herself out the front door, then ran lightly down the front walk to the street. She turned left and headed down the road, running south. It really *was* a nice day. She guessed the temperature to be in the mid-sixties. She wondered how she'd like running in snow and bitter cold when she moved up north.

As she passed by, she glanced idly at the unit Annika had mentioned. Even if she hadn't known someone new had just moved in, she wouldn't have had a problem identifying it, because there was a bunch of empty moving boxes piled up on the curb. The garage door was open and she noticed a white Corvette parked inside.

She nearly tripped.

Michael DeNiro drove a white Corvette.

Was it possible . . . ?

No.

How silly she was. The fact that their new neighbor drove a white Corvette and Michael did, too, was just a coincidence. After all, there were probably dozens of white Corvettes in the city.

Still . . . it really *was* odd.

Twenty minutes later, as she turned around and headed toward home, she was still mentally frowning, because seeing that white Corvette parked in the garage of their neighboring unit had gotten her started thinking about Michael DeNiro again, a subject she'd successfully banished from her mind since she'd last seen him in the Denny's parking lot early Tuesday morning. He hadn't been at work the past two days, which normally would have been her days off, too. So that meant he was probably on the exact same rotation she was.

She wished she'd never met him. She especially wished she'd never gone for breakfast with him.

"And why do I wish that? What's the big deal?" she muttered. She talked to herself all the time when she was running. For some reason, her brain worked better during exercise sessions.

Oh, you know why.

Her heart thumped in rhythm with her pounding feet. Yes, she thought as she rounded the corner and entered her complex. She *did* know why. She had had *fun* with Michael. She had relaxed and enjoyed herself.

The time she'd spent with Michael had underscored just exactly how regimented and confining her life had become. Work. Eat. Sleep. Run. Paint. That was her life. That's what she did. Over and over and over again.

About the only person she saw outside work was her mother. Usually once a week they'd have a meal together.

Even though everyone she knew encouraged her to get out more, to loosen up and have some fun, Shawn rarely went out, because most of her friends were other dealers or people who worked in the gambling industry, and they worked the same crazy kinds of hours she did. When they went out, it was usually after work, and mostly their entertainment consisted of hanging out in a few favorite clubs—drinking and dancing.

Shawn liked to dance, but she didn't drink much. A glass of wine was about her speed. And if you didn't drink, being around people who *were* drinking wasn't much fun. She always felt like such a prude, yet she had no intention of succumbing to the urge to be like the others.

She knew her friends thought she simply didn't approve of drinking. Shawn laughed grimly. If they only knew.

The reason Shawn didn't want to make a habit of drinking was really very simple: She was afraid to. She was afraid she had inherited her father's tendencies. She was terrified that she was just as weak and had just as addictive a personality as he did. She was also scared her judgment was as flawed as his had been.

And rather than run the risk of finding out her fears were justified, she avoided situations that might tempt her to let down her guard.

Well, she was going out tonight. She hoped it wouldn't be a waste of time.

She turned onto her street, slowing down a bit now.

As she neared the eight-unit section where her town home was located, she saw the white Corvette backing out of the garage. Within seconds, she was abreast of the car, and she stopped, waiting for it to get out of her way, but curious about its owner, too.

The window on the passenger side slid down.

"Shawn?"

Her heart shot up into her throat. Michael! She couldn't believe it. She leaned down to see inside the car. Sure enough, Michael's pleased smile greeted her.

"It *is* you," he said.

Although Shawn was stunned to see him there, she wasn't too stunned to notice his outfit—white casual pants and a black, chest-hugging T-shirt. Dark glasses covered his eyes. Probably chose his outfit to match his car, she thought contemptuously. "What are you *doing* here?" she said without smiling.

His smile faded from his face. "What do you mean by that?"

"Just what I said."

"I live here," he said slowly. "What are *you* doing here?"

She crossed her arms in front of her chest. She was still breathing hard, partly from her run, partly from her shock at seeing him there. "Don't try to pretend Liz didn't tell you I live here, too," she said sarcastically.

He stared at her for a second or two, then he turned off the ignition, opened his door, and got out of the car. He walked around until they were standing only a couple of feet apart from each other. The set of his shoulders and the tight-lipped expression on his face told her he was angry.

Very angry.

"Just what the hell is your problem, Shawn?" he

said. "I moved in here yesterday, and no, Liz didn't tell me you live here. Furthermore, why *shouldn't* I live here? It's a free country, isn't it?"

Shawn knew she had overreacted. She knew she should just let it go. But somehow she couldn't. "This isn't exactly the type of place someone like you lives in," she said flatly.

"Oh? And what type of place does *someone like me* live in?" he mimicked.

"A swinging singles pad somewhere close to town like all the other guys and most of the girls who work at the casino."

He yanked his glasses off, and now she saw exactly how angry he was. She hadn't realized golden topaz eyes could look so hard and cold. "You know, I don't know what I did to cause you to form such a low opinion of me, but I resent you passing judgment on me. I resent you deciding who and what I am without giving me a chance. You don't even *know* me, lady."

He jammed his glasses back on and, without another word, stalked around, got into his car, started it, and peeled away, burning rubber in his wake.

"Annika, what should I wear tonight?" Shawn called from her bedroom. She'd already tried on three different outfits and discarded them all. She really didn't have anything remotely suitable for a party. Especially a party at Darryl's house—a showplace in one of the nicest areas of the city.

She held a light blue dress up in front of her.

"No, no, not that one!" Annika said. "It makes you look like a schoolteacher." She leaned against the doorframe, her black silk jumpsuit draping seductively over her tall, perfectly proportioned figure. Her blond hair was twisted up into a topknot, and she'd shoved an oversize rhinestone-studded hatpin through it. On her ears dangled long rhinestone earrings.

"You make me sick," Shawn said.

Annika laughed. "Why?"

"Because you always look so *perfect*. If I wore something like that, I'd look ridiculous."

"That's because you're not tall enough to carry it off. Besides, this outfit reflects my personality, not yours," Annika said reasonably, advancing into the bedroom. She walked to Shawn's closet and rapidly looked through her clothes. "Here," she said, "this outfit." She held out a multicolored gauze skirt threaded with gold, and a matching scarf. "Just wear your dark green leotard with it, and I'll lend you my gold sandals and some long gold earrings, and you'll be all set." She smiled happily. "And I'll do your makeup and hair."

Thirty minutes later when Shawn looked in the mirror, she knew Annika had been right. She looked festive. The colors in the skirt and scarf were her colors—gold and green and pumpkin and russet. She even liked what Annika had done with her hair. Instead of its usual confinement, it billowed around Shawn's face in a cloud of soft curls. Even the makeup Annika had insisted upon didn't overwhelm Shawn's fair skin, the way it seemed to when Shawn tried applying it. No, the subtle shadings just gave her a creamy glow.

"You look wonderful," Annika said.

"Thanks." Their gazes met in the mirror.

"Hey, you never did tell me. Did you check out our new neighbor?"

Shawn grimaced. "Yeah, I checked him out."

"Well? What's he like?"

Shawn sighed. "I'm not sure." She turned. "It turns out I know him. He works at The Slipper."

"Really? Is he married?"

"Nope."

Annika frowned. "This is kind of off the beaten track for a dealer, isn't it?"

Shawn nodded. "He's not a dealer, though. He's training to be a floorman."

"Well, I want to hear all about him, but let's talk on the way. I promised Darryl we'd come early."

Shawn was driving to the party, because Annika planned to stay at Darryl's overnight. Even if she hadn't been, Shawn would probably have driven. She didn't like being stuck anywhere. If she got bored silly or got tired, she liked to be able to make a quick getaway.

As they drove slowly down the street, Shawn glanced at Michael's unit. The garage door was closed, but there were lights on inside the house.

"So come on, tell me about him," Annika said.

Ten minutes later they were halfway to Green Valley and the Legacy Golf Course, where Darryl's house was located, and Shawn had just related everything she knew about Michael and what had transpired between them since she'd met him the other night. "Anyway," she finished, "now he's mad at me."

"I can't say I blame him," Annika said quietly.

"So you think I was wrong, too?"

"Don't you?"

The quiet question disturbed Shawn, because if she were being completely truthful, she'd have to answer, yes, she deserved Michael's anger. If their roles had been reversed, she would be angry, too. Wasn't her mother always telling her not to judge people by what appeared on the surface? Just because Michael was good-looking, charming, and smooth didn't mean he was a creep, did it?

"I guess maybe I *did* overreact," she admitted.

"Honey, what you did was more than overreact," Annika said. "You were downright insulting to the man."

Shawn cringed.

"And I can't help but wonder why," Annika continued thoughtfully. "I mean, you're usually the perfect lady. It's not at all like you to be rude."

"I know . . ."

Annika was silent for a long time. Then, in a slow, speculative tone, she said, "You're *attracted* to this guy, aren't you?"

"Why do you say that?" Shawn cut a glance Annika's way.

Annika smiled. "Let's just say your behavior is so completely irrational and unlike you that there could be no other reason. You're attracted to him, and for some reason, you're scared to admit it!"

Michael stood just inside the arched doorway and surveyed the crowd of people in the enormous living room. When Jimmy Penner had mentioned the party, Michael knew it would be a good opportunity to meet more people. He'd also half hoped Shawn would be there, but now, after what had happened earlier today, he wasn't sure he really wanted to see her so soon. First he had to figure out what his next move would be.

He hadn't planned to get angry with her today. It had just happened. Something about the way she'd looked down her nose at him, as if he were lower than a slug, had made him see red.

The problem was that now he wasn't sure what to do. *Oh, hell*, he thought, *I've never forced myself on any woman, and I'm damned if I'll start now—job or no job.*

Just as the thought formed, he saw Shawn standing with a gorgeous showgirl-type blonde by the open French doors that led out to the flagstone patio and lighted pool beyond.

Wow, he thought. She looked beautiful.

As he watched her, her gaze idly swept the room. When it reached the arched doorway, it stopped and locked with his.

For a long moment, they stared at each other. All the sound in the room receded into the background. It was the strangest sensation, being in the midst of all those people and feeling as if he and Shawn were the only people in the room.

It's your move, Michael thought.

As if she'd heard him, she took a step in his direction.

Shawn's heart was beating so hard, she was sure all the people around her could hear it.

Michael wasn't smiling. Was he still angry with her? She guessed she wouldn't blame him if he was.

And why did he have to look so good? Tonight he wore tan slacks, a dark brown open-necked shirt, and a camel-colored jacket.

"Hi," she said as she finally reached his side.

"Hi."

He wasn't going to make this easy for her. "I . . . uh, I'm sorry about what I said earlier today. I was very rude. I don't blame you for being angry."

Still he said nothing.

Come on, Michael, don't make me grovel.

Then he smiled—a funny little half smile. "That's okay. I'm sorry, too."

"No, you don't have any reason to be sorry. You were right," she insisted. Now that she'd decided to apologize, she wanted to be completely fair.

He shook his head. "No. I lost my temper. And even if I was right, I shouldn't have lost my temper."

She shrugged. "Well, okay. I accept your apology." Her gaze met his, and her heart raced. She backed up, preparing to leave.

Just then the band that Darryl had hired began to play. Shawn recognized the mellow tones of "Unforgettable."

"Would you like to dance?" Michael asked.

"All right."

He put his arms around her and pulled her close. He smelled like pine forests and crisp mountain air and healthy male. Shawn closed her eyes, absorbing the sensations rushing through her. She could feel the heat of his palm against her back, the long, hard length of his body moving against hers. He was a good dancer, moving with assurance and the ease of practice.

She trembled slightly, and his arms tightened. "Is something wrong?" he murmured against her ear, his breath warm and erotic.

"No," she said.

Liar, liar.

The truth was, everything was wrong.

Because whether Shawn liked it or not, in Michael's arms, everything felt completely right.

FOUR

Damn, she felt good in his arms.

She smelled good, too—her scent a heady combination of light, flowery perfume, sweet-smelling hair, and a desirable woman.

He pulled her closer, burying his face in her coppery curls. He couldn't believe how perfectly she fit against him, her soft curves and contours matching his body exactly, as if, when she'd been created, they'd had him in mind.

The thought jolted Michael.

What had possessed him to think something like that? That kind of thinking was stupid.

Dangerous, even.

This was a woman who might be involved in something extremely illegal. His job was to find out exactly what, if anything, she had to do with the skimming operation at the casino.

And that's all.

He'd told himself before, and he guessed he'd better

tell himself again. Getting emotionally entangled with Shawn would be a big, big mistake. He simply couldn't afford to lose his objectivity.

He knew it was going to be one of the hardest jobs of his life—remembering that simple fact. Because the truth of the matter was that Shawn MacInnes, with her dreamy eyes and her bright copper curls and her innocent, untouched aura, had gotten to him.

She was the kind of woman a man wanted to put his arms around and take care of. The kind of woman who made a man think of yellow kitchens and baking bread and fat babies.

Exactly the kind of woman he had been hoping to find someday.

And wasn't that ironic? To find a woman he thought he could be serious about, and know that if he were to succumb to his feelings, he could get burned, and burned bad?

So if you know what's good for you, Vellini, you'd better cool it. Romance her, sure, if that's what it takes, but don't let it affect you. Make very damned sure you keep your emotional distance.

"Michael?"

Her soft voice shook him from his thoughts.

"The music's stopped," she said, her eyes bottomless as they gazed into his.

Michael looked around him. The music *had* stopped. In fact, he and Shawn were the only couple still on the dance floor. He laughed softly, reluctantly letting her go. "Sorry. You have a way of completely distracting me."

Color immediately stained her cheeks, and Michael thought how absolutely adorable she looked when she was embarrassed. His gaze swept her face, settling on her soft-looking lips. The urge to kiss her was so strong, he knew he'd better do or say something to take his mind off it. "Are you hungry?" he said quickly.

"A little, I guess." The becoming color had faded to a faint flush of pink.

"Why don't we go hit the buffet table, then?" He put his hand on the small of her back and guided her toward the dining room, where Darryl Anderson, their host, had obviously spared no expense.

Ten minutes later, plates of food balanced on their knees, they sat atop the brick wall that circled the large patio. Several other people similarly laden ate and chattered around them.

"This is a beautiful place, isn't it?" Shawn said after a few moments. She picked up a fat pink shrimp and ate it.

"Yes, it is," Michael said, polishing off a chicken finger. He looked around. The huge, L-shaped pool sparkled invitingly behind him, and the sand-colored stone house sprawled in front of them. Surrounded by recessed lighting, it shone like a jewel in the middle of its manicured lawns. Cactus, beautifully trimmed shrubbery, and all kinds of bright flowers Michael didn't know the names of dotted the flawless sweep of emerald lawn. It was obvious that the house and the grounds had been professionally planned and decorated.

"Annika—she's my roommate—told me Darryl's spent a fortune on everything," Shawn said. She took a bite from a small, triangular sandwich. "He's got the most successful real estate agency in Clark County."

Michael nodded. Their host amused him. He looked like an egg with his squat build and bald head, but when Michael had been introduced to him, he saw intelligence and a keen awareness in Darryl's dark eyes.

Michael recognized that look. He'd seen it before. Darryl was one of those people who understood human nature and knew exactly how to take advantage of any weaknesses a customer might possess. Michael wondered if the way Darryl dressed and talked was for effect—to lull his adversaries into thinking he was a lightweight.

Just then Michael saw their host crossing the patio, accompanied by a tall blond man who looked as if he'd just stepped from the pages of *Gentleman's Quarterly*. Darryl, however, was attired in a vivid flowing caftan and leather sandals.

"Shawn, sweetheart, *there* you are!" Darryl exclaimed in his high, squeaky voice.

Shawn set her plate down and stood. More slowly, Michael stood, too.

"I've been looking for you," Darryl said. "I wanted to introduce you to my cousin, Tod. Tod Bellamy, Shawn MacInnes." He smiled happily, rubbing his fat hands together. "She's the one I've been telling you about." He smiled at Shawn. "Tod lives in New Hampshire."

"Annika told me," Shawn said.

"It's *such* a pleasure to meet you," Tod said.

He was the kind of man Michael couldn't stand. Every blond hair in place, a perfect tan, impeccably pressed clothes, a smile that looked as if it belonged in a toothpaste ad. He probably even had his nails professionally manicured. He reminded Michael of a Ken doll.

Darryl turned to Michael. "We met earlier, didn't we? It's Michael, right?"

Michael nodded. "Yes, Michael DeNiro."

"Nice to meet you," Tod said, extending his hand

to Michael. His handshake was firm, but Michael still didn't like him. Tod promptly turned his attention and his smile back to Shawn.

"So are you enjoying your visit to Vegas?" she said, smiling up at him.

Tod's smile expanded, if such a thing were possible. "Yes, very much. Darryl tells me you're thinking of moving up to my area of the country."

"Yes," she answered. "I am. Hopefully sometime next summer."

"That's great!" Tod gushed. "Have you picked a place yet?"

"Not yet. I'm thinking about Maine or Vermont, though."

"Great!" Tod said again. "Maybe we can get together later and talk. I'd love—"

"She's going to be busy later." Michael put his arm around Shawn possessively and held her firmly against him. He thought how much he'd like to punch out Smiling Tod's lights.

Tod blinked.

Shawn stared at Michael, astonishment written all over her face.

Michael stared back.

Darryl cleared his throat. "Uh . . . well, Tod? Listen, there's . . . uh . . . somebody else inside that I really want you to meet." He took his cousin's arm, winked at Michael, and led Tod off. "Have fun, you two," he sang out over Tod's protests.

Shawn extricated herself from Michael's grip.

Michael braced himself for what he was sure would be an angry reprimand.

She surprised him. She grinned, a teasing twinkle in

her eyes. "Do you suppose the color of Tod's hair is natural?" she asked.

Relief flooded Michael, and he grinned back. "Of course. He's probably one of those perfect guys who never even sweats."

She giggled. It was an enchanting sound. "I'll bet he doesn't have hair on his chest, either." As soon as the words were out of her mouth, she looked shocked. "I can't believe I said that!" Then she giggled again.

"Shawn . . ." At that moment, he wanted nothing more than to gather her in his arms and kiss her senseless.

Her laughter died as she met his gaze. He wondered if his thoughts showed in his eyes.

"What?" she said softly.

He touched her cheek lightly. It felt like rose petals— soft and delicate. "Let's blow this joint," he murmured.

For a long moment she didn't say anything. A breeze lifted her hair, and her fragrance drifted toward him. Michael could feel his heart beating.

Finally she sighed. A soft smile curved her lips. "Okay."

They didn't tell anyone good-bye. Within minutes Michael was following her winking taillights and wondering how in God's name he was ever going to stick to his resolution to keep his feelings for Shawn objective.

All the way home Shawn tried to figure out what was happening to her. When she had first seen Michael standing across the crowded room, all she had intended to do was walk over to him, tell him she was sorry for being so rude earlier, and walk away.

Instead she had danced with him, sat and eaten with

him, let him act as if he owned her, and now she'd left with him.

So what next? she wondered. It was obvious that whatever she told herself she was going to do wouldn't necessarily be what she'd end up doing. Because when she was within ten feet of Michael, she forgot everything. All her good resolutions, all her commonsense arguments, all her objectivity, vanished like the morning mist when the sun came up.

There was just something about Michael she couldn't resist.

Didn't even *want* to resist.

Every few minutes she glanced into her rearview mirror to see if he was still following her.

He was.

Before long they were turning in to their town house complex. Within minutes she had reached her unit and driven around the back, where she opened the garage door with her remote control. By the time she'd pulled her Honda into her parking slot, she heard Michael's footsteps.

He waited just outside the garage.

Heart quickening, she walked out to meet him.

The cool night air surrounded them. Crickets sang, and a full moon shone down from the navy night. Out here it was quiet, and the lights of the Strip and downtown casinos seemed far away. Somewhere close by an owl hooted, followed by a burst of song from a mockingbird.

"Are you going to invite me in?" he asked.

She hesitated, trying to hang on to some semblance of good sense.

"I'd invite you to my place, but knowing how proper you are, I figured you'd turn me down."

"I would have." She still should, she thought. After all, it was just as dangerous to have him at her place as it would be to go to his. If Annika were coming home, it might be different, but just knowing they would have complete, uninterrupted privacy was asking for trouble. She raised her eyes to meet his gaze. "All right. Come on in."

While Michael walked around the living room and looked at the paintings hanging on the walls, Shawn put on a pot of coffee. She had half a cheesecake in the refrigerator, and took it out. When everything was ready she carried a tray into the living room.

She still didn't know why she'd asked him in. She didn't understand herself at all.

He had taken his jacket off and was standing in front of her favorite painting. Painted in a quasi-impressionist style, it was Shawn's rendering of an old woman she'd seen in Lorenzi Park. The woman had been sitting in a wheelchair at the edge of a clearing, and she'd been watching a group of youngsters play kickball. Her wizened face had had such a look of wistfulness upon it. She had touched Shawn deeply, and she'd immediately taken a couple of pictures of her.

"This is good," Michael said. "Really good."

"Thank you." Something warm settled into her stomach at his quiet praise.

He walked over to another, smaller painting—this one of a weary-looking pregnant mother holding the hands of two toddlers. "I like the way you do these portraits," he said. "The hazy background and the rich colors in the foreground are very effective."

She smiled, pleased. He'd said he knew a little about art, but even if Michael didn't know anything, she had obviously given him pleasure. In addition to communicating her feelings to others, giving pleasure was always an objective. Of course, she also wanted to be able to support herself with her painting, and maybe one day soon she would.

Later, after they'd each had a cup of coffee and a piece of cheesecake, Michael fixed himself a second cup of coffee and said, "You know, I've been thinking about what you said this morning."

Shawn grimaced. "I wish you'd forget about that."

"Well, the thing is, I don't blame you for thinking what you thought." When she would have said something, he held up his hand. "Wait. Hear me out."

She sighed. "Okay."

"Believe me, Shawn, I understand your reluctance to get involved with someone who works in the industry, especially since you plan to leave Las Vegas as soon as you can. But I have no intention of staying in this business one day longer than I have to, either."

Shawn prided herself on her ability to recognize when someone was telling the truth. Michael was telling the truth. She'd stake her life on it. She nodded slowly. "What are you planning to do?"

"I'm planning to open a restaurant."

"A restaurant?"

He gave her a quizzical look. "Why do you sound so surprised?"

She shrugged. "I don't know. I just . . . well, do you *know* anything about the restaurant business?"

"Sure. The whole time I was in college I worked in a restaurant."

"College?" For some reason, his disclosure took her aback.

"Yeah, I . . . uh . . . I studied business." For the

first time since she'd met him, he seemed a little flustered, almost embarrassed.

"Oh, I see." She didn't see at all, but she waited for him to explain. Why was he embarrassed? Then it dawned on her. Maybe he hadn't done well in school. He'd probably never graduated, and he was embarrassed to admit it. That must be it. "Well," she said hurriedly, wanting to put him at ease again, "when do you think you'll reach your goal? It must cost an awful lot of money to open a restaurant."

"It does. But I've been saving every penny I can, and maybe by next summer I'll be realizing my dream just as you're realizing yours." His voice was fired with enthusiasm.

Saving every penny he could? With the clothes he wore and the car he drove?

"Why are you frowning?" he asked.

Shawn hadn't realized she *was* frowning. "I . . . oh, never mind."

He cocked his head. "What?"

She hesitated. "It's really none of my business."

Now he frowned and leaned forward. "Hey, come on. Now you've got my curiosity aroused. What's bothering you?"

"Well . . ." Oh, rats. He'd *asked*. "I don't know . . . it's just that you said you've been saving every penny, and you, well, you wear such expensive clothes, and your car . . ." Her voice trailed off.

"Oh, that. Well, my father has quite a bit of money, and he likes to buy me things," he said smoothly.

Almost too smoothly, Shawn thought.

"He doesn't want me to open a restaurant. He wants me to take over his business, so he likes tempting me with expensive presents. I guess he thinks I'll get used to them and give up my idea." He laughed. "I won't, which he'll eventually have to accept. Like it or not."

Now, *that* definitely had the ring of truth, Shawn thought, and she relaxed. What was wrong with her, doubting everything Michael said? "What kind of business is your father in?"

"Let's just say he wheels and deals." He grimaced. "He's always trying to bribe me. He even bought me a Rolex watch last Christmas, but I refuse to wear the damned thing. I'd probably get mugged for it."

Shawn nodded. "You don't really have to worry much about muggings in Las Vegas, you know. At least not around the casinos."

"No? Why not?"

"Because the city fathers are paranoid about the tourists. Tourists are what keep us going, and if they get scared to come here—especially the high rollers—we'd be in deep trouble. So we take extra good care of our visitors and make sure they don't get mugged. It's very rare that a hotel room is broken into, as well. Security is extra tight at all times. At least around the casinos."

"That's good," Michael said. "What about out here?"

"This complex has great security," Shawn assured him. In fact, that was one of the reasons she and Annika had wanted to live here. "But back to your restaurant. Are you going to open it here?"

"No. I've picked out a spot around the Saratoga area in upstate New York." He leaned back in his chair and crossed his legs, resting one ankle on the other knee. "I love it there. It's beautiful country. That's where my mother was from."

"Is that where your parents live now?"

"No. My father lives in New York City. My mother's

dead.'' A bleakness clouded his eyes momentarily. "She died of breast cancer when she was fifty-six.'' He grimaced. "Sometimes I still find it hard to believe she's gone, and it's been three years.''

"I understand,'' Shawn said softly. "I lost my father seven years ago, and there are still times when I think, oh, gosh, I've got to call Dad and tell him about this.'' She smiled grimly, swallowing against the painful lump in her throat. "Then, of course, I remember.'' She looked down at her hands. Why did it still hurt so much? she wondered. Was it because her father had taken his life? Deliberately left her mother and her to face not only the shock of his death, but his mountain of debts as well?

For a long moment they didn't talk. A quiet understanding flowed between them.

"What about your mother?'' he asked. "Does she live here?''

"Yes.''

"Are you close to her?''

Shawn smiled. "Very close. My mother's really wonderful. She's strong and positive and doesn't believe in dwelling on things you can't change. She has a little dance studio near downtown. When she was younger, she danced with one of the big shows here in Vegas.''

Michael grinned. "So that's where you get your gorgeous legs.''

Shawn could feel herself blushing again. "I don't have gorgeous legs,'' she said hurriedly.

"Yes, you do.'' All the sadness had disappeared from his eyes. Now they were filled with teasing glints.

What was it about Michael that made her feel this way? Why did he, of all the men she'd met over the past few years, make her feel so much like a woman? And so aware of the fact that she was desirable?

Because he makes no secret of the fact that he desires you, that's why. Flustered, Shawn looked away, saying, "You said your father lives in New York City?"

When she looked up again, Michael had a knowing look in his eyes, as if to say, *you're not fooling me, you know. I know you're trying to change the subject.* To her intense relief, though, he didn't push her. "Yes."

"Is that where you grew up?"

"Sort of. We lived on Long Island."

"How'd you end up here? If you wanted to work in a casino, why not go to Atlantic City?"

Michael shrugged. "My father has connections here. And things are tough back east. Not a lot of jobs available."

Shawn grinned. "Even if I hadn't known you weren't a native of Vegas, that remark would have given you away."

"What remark?"

" 'Connections.' No one says they have connections here. Everyone says 'juice.' Like, 'he's got a lot of juice.' " She idly picked at a loose thread in her skirt. "Sometimes I get so sick of hearing about this person's juice or that person's juice. Everyone's so hung up on power and money here."

"People are hung up on power and money *everywhere*," he said cynically. "That's all most people think about."

"Oh, Michael, don't destroy my illusions. Are you saying that even if I move to some little town in New England, I won't escape that kind of thing?"

He shrugged. "Maybe you'll be lucky." His expression said he didn't think so.

"Before I get any more depressed, let's change the subject. Tell me about the rest of your family. Do you have any brothers or sisters?"

"Yes, I've got an older sister. Well, she's only three years older, but you'd think she was my mother the way she orders me around and worries about me."

"It must be nice to have a sister," Shawn said wistfully.

"It is. Rosemary's great. She's married to a great guy and they live in the San Francisco area. She and Don have got a couple of kids, and they seem really happy." He paused, then added thoughtfully, "Sometimes I'm jealous of her."

Shawn knew what he meant. When she saw a young family together, she felt the same way, wondering if she'd ever meet anyone she could commit herself to. If she'd ever have the kind of life she dreamed of. "It's nice that you have a sister, though. I'm an only child."

He laughed. "There were times when Rosemary got so bossy, I wished I *was* an only child."

Shawn knew he wasn't serious. She could see how he felt about his sister in the way he talked about her.

"Do you see her very often?" she asked.

"I try to get out there at least twice a year. And she comes east a couple of times a year. We're always together for the holidays."

"What about this year? Will your family come here?"

He looked startled, as if he hadn't thought about it. "I really don't know."

They talked for a while longer, then he said, "Luis tells me your uncle is the head pit boss at The Slipper."

"Yes."

"What's he like?"

"Haven't you met him yet?" she asked.

"Nope. But I'd like to."

"You will. He makes it a point to rotate shifts so that he works with all the employees." She smiled. "You'll like him, I think. He's a nice guy. He and my mother are engaged to be married."

"Oh?"

Just then the little clock on the mantel chimed the hour, and Shawn looked up. It was midnight.

Michael looked at the clock, too. "It's getting late, isn't it?" He stood. "Maybe I'd better get going." Smiling, he added, "Don't want to overstay my welcome, especially now since you've decided I might not be such a bad guy, after all."

"I never thought you were a bad guy," Shawn protested. She stood, too.

"Of course you did." Now the teasing twinkle was back in his eyes. He picked up his jacket and put it on. "You made it real clear exactly what you thought."

"I'm sorry."

"It's okay. I don't hold a grudge." He walked toward the foyer, and she slowly followed him. He turned to face her, and she stopped a couple of feet away. Suddenly she felt awkward and unsure of herself again, especially when his soft brown gaze met hers. "I enjoyed this," he said. "The coffee and cheesecake and conversation. Thanks."

"You're welcome." Why couldn't she ever think of anything clever to say?

"Shawn . . ." He took a step closer.

Shawn wanted to back up. Actually, for one terrified moment, she wanted to turn tail and run. But she didn't. She met his gaze squarely, thinking, he's going to kiss me.

A moment later, his hands settled on her shoulders.

Shawn swallowed hard. Her heart picked up speed, and all she could think of was that things were moving entirely too fast. She wasn't sure she even wanted to see Michael again, let alone be kissed by him.

"Don't look so scared," he said softly. "I just want to kiss you good night. Is that okay?"

Wordlessly, as if her body were being controlled by someone other than her, she nodded.

Eyes gleaming, he gently pulled her closer. Shawn lifted her face, and as his mouth descended, she closed her eyes. His warm lips settled against hers, tasting faintly of cheesecake and coffee. Her heart fluttered wildly as slowly, and very softly, he explored her mouth, brushing his lips this way and that. His hand slid around and up into her hair, holding her head firmly against his. Then he turned his head slightly, deepening the kiss. Shawn felt light-headed from the sensations he was causing. Suddenly nothing else existed except Michael: the smell of him, the feel of him, and the taste of him. She knew she should push him away, but she didn't want to.

The kiss lasted a long time. When he finally released her, Shawn felt as if she had just fallen from a great height. There was an odd curling sensation in her belly, and her knees felt weak.

"When am I going to see you again?" His voice sounded rough and uneven.

"I don't know." He looked as if he were going to kiss her again, and she wasn't sure she could handle another kiss with that much voltage. She backed up, suddenly frightened of her strong reaction to him. Confusion eddied through her.

He reached for her again. "Shawn, I—"

She put her hands against his chest. "No, Michael, please. Things are moving too fast. I . . . I need some time to think."

His hands dropped. He studied her silently for a minute. "How much time?"

"I don't know." He was probably going to get very sick of hearing those three words.

Very gently, he touched the tip of her nose. "While you're deciding, I want you to remember something."

Shawn was mesmerized by the expression in his eyes.

"I think you're pretty special," he said softly.

"Michael—"

His finger moved from her nose to her lips. "Shh," he said. "Don't say anything else. Just think about what I said." He dropped a light kiss on her mouth. "I'll see you tomorrow."

And then he left.

FIVE

At ten minutes to five the following afternoon, Shawn climbed the steps leading to her mother's dance studio. Even before she reached the door, she could hear the thump, thump, thump of ballerina-slipper-clad feet and the rhythmic voice of her mother as she counted. "One, two, three, four . . ."

Shawn peered through the swirled glass door. Today's class looked fairly well advanced in skill level, and most of the girls seemed to be around the age of fourteen or older. She smiled as she saw how fiercely they were concentrating on their moves, how closely they listened to her mother's commands, how committed and serious they seemed.

If they were still taking dance at this age, they *were* serious, Carolyn MacInnes had once explained. Almost all of them pictured themselves as professional dancers sometime in the future. Very few would make it, but Carolyn didn't believe in discouraging anyone.

"Who am I to rain on anyone's parade?" she had

asked Shawn, and Shawn agreed. Everyone should be allowed to have their dreams. Without dreams, life wouldn't be worth living.

She should know. She'd existed on dreams for years.

Finally the dance was over, and Shawn opened the door. Her mother looked up, pleasure lighting her face when she recognized Shawn. "Well, hi, honey! This is a nice surprise!" They hugged briefly. "What're you doing here?" her mother said as they pulled apart.

"I had some errands to run. Anyway, I was over this way, so I just thought I'd stop by. Isn't this your last class today?"

"Yes. In five minutes we'll be through." Carolyn clapped her hands. "All right, girls. Line up at the barre and do your cool-down for five minutes."

The dozen or so girls slowly filed to the barre and began their routine. Carolyn inclined her head toward the end of the long room, where her small office was located. "Why don't you go sit down? I'll be with you in a few minutes."

Shawn admired her mother's lithe figure as she walked away. Although Carolyn was fifty-three years old, her body could have belonged to a woman half her age. She was clad in a black leotard and tights, showing her beautiful legs with their well-defined calf muscles to advantage.

Shawn smiled, thinking about Michael's remark the previous evening. Her mother *did* have great legs, and if Shawn was truthful—at least to herself—she'd admit that she did, too. Her one better-than-average asset, something she'd never really appreciated when she was younger. Of course, since she avoided the sun, so rarely wore a bathing suit, and wasn't the type to wear mini-skirts, she hardly ever got a chance to show off her legs. Not that she wanted to, but . . .

Shawn shook herself. There she went again, off on a tangent. Honestly. She'd spent more time mooning around today, thinking about Michael and the way she'd felt when he'd kissed her last night. Actually, she'd been reliving the kiss, over and over again. She'd spent so much time thinking and remembering, she hadn't been able to concentrate on her painting today, and she'd been unhappy with her efforts.

If this was what it was like to have a man interested in you, she thought in disgust, well, maybe she'd been luckier than she'd thought *not* to be like her friends.

When her mother joined her a little later, the first thing she said was, "Is something on your mind, or is this just a plain old visit?" She smoothed back her dark hair, which didn't really need smoothing, since it was confined in a neat chignon. Her eyes, the same clear blue as Shawn's, rested on Shawn's face.

"It's a plain old visit," Shawn lied. She was not going to tell her mother about Michael. That would be making much more of the kiss . . . and him . . . than Shawn was willing to make of them. "I was hoping maybe we could have dinner together."

Carolyn frowned. "Oh, honey, I wish I could, but Philip is coming over."

"Oh." Shawn tried not to feel disappointed. She was glad her mother had found happiness with her uncle Philip, glad they were engaged to be married at Christmastime, glad her mother had someone to depend on . . . but sometimes she couldn't suppress a tiny prickle of jealousy. She and her mother had been so close for so long, fought so many battles together. Now Carolyn had someone else to confide in, and Shawn couldn't help feeling like an outsider. Shawn didn't like herself when these feelings surfaced, but as long as she was careful to keep Carolyn from knowing she had them, she guessed they were harmless. And normal.

She forced a cheery smile to her face. "Well, some other time then . . ."

"Listen, why don't you come home with me?" Carolyn said brightly. "You can have dinner with us. Philip would love that, I know. He said just the other day that we don't see enough of you."

"Oh, I don't think so. . . ."

"Why not? You're not still on swing swift, are you?"

"No, I start the night shift tonight."

"Good. That's settled. You're coming home with me. But we don't have to hurry off. Philip's not due until eight. And I'm parched. How about if we have a cup of tea first? Then we can head for the house." Carolyn kept a pot on the hot plate at all times.

Shawn nodded.

As Carolyn made their tea, she said, "So what's going on with you? Met any interesting guys lately?"

Shawn willed herself not to blush, but she could feel her cheeks heating even as she said, "Why do you always ask that question?"

Carolyn laughed as she handed Shawn a cup of tea. "Don't you know it's a mother's mission in life to see that her daughter is happily married?" Then she looked at Shawn more closely. Her eyes widened. "'Is that a *blush* I see? Shawn! It is! You *have* met someone."

"No, not really—"

"Shawn Carolyn MacInnes, don't you lie to me!"

Carolyn sat down behind her desk and sipped her tea while eyeing Shawn speculatively.

Shawn sighed. Why had she come here today? Had she secretly *wanted* to tell her mother about Michael? "Oh, okay. Yes, I have met someone." When Carolyn said nothing, just sat expectantly, Shawn frowned. "I don't think there's any future in it, though."

"Why don't you start from the beginning? Tell me who he is, how you met him, and why you think there's no future in it." Suddenly alarm flashed in her mother's eyes. "He's not *married*, is he?"

"No! At least . . ." Shawn frowned. "No, I'm sure he's not married."

Carolyn sank back in her swivel chair. "Well, that's a relief." She grinned. "So come on, tell me all about him."

"There's really not much to tell."

"Try."

Oh, come on. Isn't that the real reason you came today? Because you wanted to tell her about Michael?

"He's a new floorman. I met him the other night. His name is Michael DeNiro. We had breakfast together when the shift was over. And now, as it turns out, he's living in the same town house complex. We ran into each other last night at a party at Darryl Anderson's house and ended up going home together." She stated this last piece of information very casually, as if it were not the least bit important to her. Still elaborately casual, she met her mother's thoughtful gaze. "There. Satisfied? Now you know all there is to know."

"You still haven't told me why you think there's no future in it," Carolyn said quietly.

Darn. Why had she ever said that in the first place? She should have known her mother wouldn't let it die.

Shawn shrugged. "I don't know. It's just a feeling I have. Forget I said anything about it."

"Shawn . . ."

As she searched for the right words, Shawn traced a pattern on her embroidered cotton skirt. "I'm probably being silly, but he's very eastern-seaboard-sophisticated and smooth. He's not my type. He's the type to go after someone like Annika," she finished softly. She wanted to add that he reminded her too much of her father, but she knew an admission like that would hurt her mother.

Carolyn sat forward, frowning, and set her teacup down. "You say he's not your type, yet you are obviously attracted to him."

"Yes, I am." She met her mother's gaze. "But just because a person wants something doesn't mean it's good for her, does it?"

"No, but how will you know if you don't take a chance?"

"I thought you didn't believe in gambling," Shawn countered.

"Normally I don't. But relationships are different. You have to take chances there."

"Mom . . . do . . . do you ever regret marrying Dad?"

Sadness flitted through her mother's eyes and she looked away. When she turned back to Shawn, the sadness was gone, and her gaze was once again steady and calm. "No, honey, I don't."

"Not even after what he did to you?" How could her mother look so serene? Shawn's own heart was twisted with pain.

"No. I'm sorry about what happened, of course. I wish your father had been stronger. I wish he could have stuck around and faced his problems. And I'm sorry he hurt *you* so much, but sorry I married him? Never!''

Shawn wanted to believe her mother. Wanted to believe that there were no secret regrets. Wanted to believe that all the heartache and pain had been worth it.

"If I hadn't married your father, honey, I wouldn't have had you," Carolyn added softly. "For that reason alone, it was worth it."

Shawn blinked back sudden tears.

"I loved your father. And despite what happened in the end, we had a lot of good years. I'm not sorry about any of them. And I don't want you to be, either."

Shawn bit her bottom lip and stared at her clasped hands. If only she could be like her mother. If only she could forgive so easily. Forgive and forget.

"Shawn . . ."

Shawn raised her eyes. "What?"

Carolyn's clear blue gaze met hers steadily. "Honey, don't let what happened with me and your father ruin your life."

"What makes you think that'll happen?"

"I can see the signs of it happening already, even if you can't."

"Just because I've got high standards—"

"It's more than high standards. It seems to me that you judge every man by what your father did. That's not healthy." Her mother's eyes seemed to see clear down to Shawn's soul.

Shawn squirmed in her chair. She drank the rest of her tea and avoided her mother's gaze.

"So tell me about this Michael," her mother said after awhile.

"I already did."

"Shawn . . ."

Shawn sighed. "All right, all right. He's in his early thirties, I think, and he's very attractive in a predatory sort of way."

Carolyn frowned.

"Oh, don't get alarmed. Actually, he's very nice and he's a lot of fun to be with. Easy to talk to."

Carolyn smiled. "He sounds wonderful. What's your problem?"

"I don't know. It's just a feeling I have. I can't put a name to it. It's been bugging me for days."

"What kind of feeling?"

"You're going to think I'm being melodramatic, but there's something about him that just doesn't add up."

Carolyn waited quietly.

Shawn told her about Michael's plans to go into the restaurant business. "And he said he'd been saving his money and would soon have enough."

"Well, that sounds pretty ambitious and admirable."

"It does doesn't it? But he drives a Corvette and wears expensive clothes." Shawn fiddled with the aquamarine birthstone ring on her left hand. "And when I said something to him about the car and everything, he said his father had money and liked to buy him expensive things."

"Sounds reasonable to me," her mother said.

"I thought so at the time. But since then I've thought about something else. Why is he living in a two-bedroom town house when he could live in a much cheaper one-bedroom apartment?"

"*You* live in a town house instead of an apartment," Carolyn pointed out.

"I know, but that's different."

"How is it different?"

"Well, for one thing, I have a roommate, so my cost

is the same as it would be if I lived alone in a small apartment.''

"That's true.'' Carolyn pursed her lips. "If that bothers you, Shawn, why don't you just ask him?''

Shawn grimaced. "I'm sure if I asked him, he'd have a ready answer. Something that makes perfect sense.'' She sighed heavily. "Oh, shoot. It sounds ridiculous, doesn't it? I'm probably making something out of nothing, but . . . I don't know . . . it just doesn't *feel* right.'' She bit her bottom lip, then said slowly, "He's been to college. He said so. So what's he doing working in a casino as a floorman?''

"Now, Shawn, you know perfectly well there are a lot of ex-teachers working in casinos because they can make more money there.''

"I know.'' Why was she still questioning Michael's motives and the things he'd told her? As her mother had said, they sounded perfectly reasonable.

Her mother sat thinking for a few minutes, obviously mulling over what Shawn had told her. "Tell you what. Why don't you ask Philip to check Michael's employment file?''

Shawn stared at her mother. "Can he do that?''

"Certainly. He's the head pit boss, isn't he? He has a perfect right to ask about people in his own division.''

Shawn nodded slowly.

Carolyn smiled. "Good. That should put your mind at rest. Talk to Philip about it tonight.''

"It seems kind of underhanded, doesn't it? And what if Uncle Philip doesn't want to do it?''

"Don't worry about that. Just ask him. If he doesn't want to, he can say no. But I don't think he will. He's just as concerned about you and your welfare as I am.''

Shawn wasn't sure it was right to check up on Michael.

She knew she wouldn't like it if he did the same thing to her. But she pushed down her misgivings. Her mother didn't seem to think there was anything wrong with investigating to see if he'd told her the truth. Besides, if Michael *had* told her the truth about everything, he'd never have to know she'd checked up on him. And if he hadn't . . . well . . . then she didn't care *what* he thought.

Michael tapped his foot impatiently as he listened to the phone ringing in his father's apartment. He checked his watch. Almost seven. He'd been trying to reach his father all afternoon. Why didn't someone answer? Where the hell was Yolanda, his housekeeper? And if they were both out, why didn't the answering service pick up?

Just as Michael was ready to hang up, his father's breathless voice said, "Hello?"

"Hi, Dad. It's Michael. You sound out of breath."

"I *am* out of breath. I was in the shower."

Michael grinned at the irritated tone. "Sorry. But I've been calling you all day. And why didn't Yolanda get the phone?"

"I gave Yolanda the day off. But never mind that. How is everything going? Have you made any progress?"

"By progress, if you mean do I know who's stealing from the casino yet, no, I don't. But everything is proceeding according to plan. I've identified all the suspects on the list and met most of them, including Shawn MacInnes."

"Good, good. What's your impression of her?"

Michael hesitated. "Frankly, it's difficult to believe she's involved in this in any way."

"It's kind of early to make a judgment like that,

don't you think?'' Victor said. "You barely know the woman.'' Then he laughed. "Oh, I see. You're not letting yourself be swayed by the fact that she's pretty, are you?''

"How do *you* know she's pretty?''

"An educated guess.''

"You know, Dad, if I'd said I thought she was involved, you'd never have questioned my judgment. It's only because I've said I don't think she's a part of this that you're skeptical.''

"Maybe.'' But Victor didn't sound convinced. "However,'' he added, "be warned. Don't allow your lower anatomy to rule your brain, Michael. Romance the woman if you must, but don't ever forget what your job is and why you're there.''

Michael clenched his jaw. "Have I ever forgotten? Ever let you down? Even once?''

"No.''

"Then why would you say a thing like that? You don't have to tell me how to do my job.''

"I'm sorry, Michael. You're right.'' Victor sighed, the sound clearly audible over the phone. "It's been a long day, and I'm tired, otherwise I never would have said what I said.''

Sure, Michael thought. Sometimes his father exasperated him, but Michael knew Victor would never change.

"So what about Philip Brownlee? Have you met him yet?''

"No, not yet, but I hope to soon.''

"Dominic tells me Brownlee gives the appearance of being a very hard worker. He said he's also impressed with Brownlee's knowledge of the casino business and his apparent loyalty to The Glass Slipper. But I'll be interested in hearing what you think.''

"Well," Michael said, "I'll let you know as soon as I have a chance to talk to him. But right now, I'd better go. It's time for me to leave for work. I'll call you again in a day or so."

For the rest of the evening Michael thought about his conversation with his father. He'd wanted to tell Victor that Shawn wasn't like any other woman he'd ever met. That she was more than just pretty. That there was a special innocence, a sincerity and integrity, about her that Michael couldn't believe was faked. Yet something had held Michael back, because there was a tiny part of him that wondered if his judgment *was* unbiased. He wondered what his father would think if he knew how Michael had been thinking of Shawn all day long. How he'd kept remembering the delicious feel of her soft lips under his, the warmth of her mouth, and the sweet curves of her body.

How can you be totally impartial when you're so attracted to her?

The question reverberated in his mind. Was his father right?

No, dammit. Victor *wasn't* right. The first time Michael had seen Shawn, his gut instinct had told him she couldn't be a part of the skimming operation. And unless he'd completely lost his ability to read a person's character, he *still* believed she wasn't. In fact, the more he was around Shawn, the more convinced he was that she wasn't involved.

And his attraction to her had nothing whatsoever to do with this conviction.

*   *   *

The sound of the doorbell ringing reverberated through the small ranch house where Shawn had grown up.

"Honey, would you let Philip in?" Carolyn said as she opened the oven and poked at the casserole inside.

Shawn headed toward the front door.

"Hi, Shawn! I didn't expect to see you here." Philip Brownlee's face held a pleased smile. He walked inside and leaned down to kiss Shawn's cheek.

"Hi," Shawn said. "Mom invited me for dinner. I hope you don't mind."

"Mind? Why should I mind? I don't see enough of you, so I don't mind at all," he said.

She smiled up at him, thinking that he had aged well and was better-looking than he'd been in his younger days. His brown hair was heavily salted with gray, but it was still thick and healthy-looking. His hazel eyes, behind horn-rimmed glasses, were sharp and intelligent. He was an avid golfer, playing nearly every day, so his body was trim and deeply tanned from the desert sun.

Philip Brownlee was her half uncle, if such a thing existed. Her father and Philip had the same mother, but different fathers. Shawn had always been very fond of him.

At sixty-two, Philip was seven years older than Gerald would have been, not nearly as handsome or personable, and much more serious, but there was something very solid and dependable about him, she thought.

He'd been like a rock after Gerald's death, helping Carolyn with all the problems that had arisen, acting as a buffer between her and irate creditors. And then, of course, he'd completely settled the remainder of Gerald's debts when he'd supposedly come into some money from a great-aunt whom Carolyn and Shawn hadn't even known existed. Shawn still wondered if Philip hadn't made up that story because he knew Carolyn's pride wouldn't have allowed her to take his money.

Shawn was grateful to him for everything he'd done for her mother, yet something held her back from complete devotion, and she didn't quite understand what it was. She'd never said anything to her mother about her feelings; Shawn was mature enough to realize that Carolyn deserved whatever happiness she could find. Still, complete acceptance of Philip seemed like a betrayal of her father.

Shawn had also told herself many times that Gerald had forfeited his right to her loyalty. After all, he betrayed both her and her mother, but she still couldn't completely accept Philip in his place. She knew this was her problem, something she would have to deal with, and she'd vowed not to give her mother any indication that she was less than one hundred percent happy for her.

"Mm, something smells good," Philip said as he and Shawn entered the kitchen.

Carolyn turned from the stove, lifting her face for his kiss, her eyes soft and welcoming.

Shawn looked away.

"Fix yourself a drink," Carolyn said as she resumed her stirring. "And talk to Shawn while I finish up dinner."

Philip complied, going unerringly to the cabinet where Carolyn stored her liquor, obviously completely at home in her mother's house. "Let's go out to the living room," he suggested to Shawn.

"But don't you need some help?" Shawn asked her mother.

Carolyn shook her head. "No. Everything's almost ready. You two go talk." She gave Shawn a pointed look. "Ask him about Michael."

"Who's Michael?" Philip asked as he and Shawn settled themselves on the russet couch in the living room.

"Michael DeNiro. He's one of the new floormen at The Slipper."

"Yes, I recognize the name now."

Shawn explained how she and Michael had met, and told Philip most of what she'd told Carolyn, leaving out the more personal details. "Anyway, Mom suggested that you could look at his employee file and let me know if he's told me the truth."

Philip frowned. "I haven't met him yet, but sometimes weeks go by before I meet someone new. It depends on the shift they're working."

Shawn nodded.

"But I'll check him out."

"You're sure you don't mind?"

Philip smiled. "Are you kidding? Of course I don't mind. In fact, if *you're* interested in him, I'd want to check him out for my *own* satisfaction." He reached out and took her hand. "Your happiness and future well-being are as important to me as they are to your mother. You know that, don't you?"

Shawn gave him a grateful smile, and she tried to ignore the ache in her heart. The ache that said if only her father had felt the same way, he might be here tonight, where he belonged.

When Shawn reported for work at midnight, the first person she saw was Michael. Their gazes met for the briefest of moments, and he smiled. Pleasure surged through her in a warm rush, and she quickly looked away.

For the remainder of the shift she was constantly aware of him. Even when he was at the opposite end of the pit, she could see his dark head. Her awareness of him kept her edgy—a mixture of emotions that was part nerves, part excitement, part anticipation.

She wondered if he'd thought about last night as much as she had. He had said he thought she was special. Had she meant that, or was that just something he said, part of his line, a way to soften her up for the kill?

She wanted to believe Michael was sincere. Wanted to believe that tender look in his eyes had been for real and not part of his practiced charm. Just thinking about the look in his eyes when he'd said good-bye had her stomach all tied up in knots.

What would he think if he knew she'd asked her uncle to check him out? Would he be angry? Or amused? It was a moot point, she thought, because he never *would* find out.

She also wondered what he'd say or how he'd act when they finally had a chance to talk today. Part of her couldn't wait to be with him. The other part of her was scared to death. When her first break time came, she swallowed nervously as she walked toward the employee lounge. But then she saw Michael talking with Jimmy Penner and she realized he wasn't on the same break schedule tonight. Relief mixed with disappointment arrowed through her.

She pushed open the door to the lounge and spied Liz in front of one of the vending machines. After getting herself a soft drink, she and Liz sat at one of the small tables. "Where'd you take off to last night?" Liz said, breaking open her bag of barbecued corn chips and popping some into her mouth. "I saw you with Michael-the-hunk, then the next thing I knew, the two of you were gone."

"I got bored and went home." It wasn't a *complete* lie. She *had* gone home.

Liz smiled slyly. "Shawn, dear heart, you're blushing again."

"I am not!" But Shawn knew she was. She could feel the heat in her cheeks. Darn. She was such a poor liar.

Liz's smile expanded. "You went home with Michael-the-hunk, didn't you?"

"Will you quit calling him that?"

"Will you quit evading my question?"

Shawn sighed. "Yes, Michael followed me home, and he came in for a while."

"My, my. Things are progressing awfully fast, aren't they? Now, aren't you glad I invited him to Denny's the other morning?" Liz ate some more chips and drank some of her cola. "And you tried to pretend you weren't interested in him!"

Shawn knew it would be useless to answer. Instead she decided to counterattack. "I saw *you* with Jimmy."

Liz grinned again. "Yeah. He and Candy broke up, y'know."

"No, I didn't know." Candy was one of the cocktail waitresses, and she and Jimmy Penner had been an item for months.

"Well, they did. And Jimmy's been giving me the eye for a while. So last night we ended up at his place." Liz leaned closer and said sotto voce, "He's great in bed."

"Liz!"

Liz laughed out loud.

Shawn knew she was blushing again. She hated when Liz talked so openly about her sex life, and Liz knew she hated it.

"What about Michael? Is he good in bed?"

"Liz!" Shawn said again. "I barely know him. I didn't go to bed with him." She didn't mean to sound judgmental. In fact, she wasn't. What Liz did was her business. Shawn was just uncomfortable hearing about it.

"I can't believe you didn't *think* about it," Liz insisted slyly. "God, he's such a hunk. How could you *not* think about it?" She grinned again. "I wouldn't have been able to think about anything else!"

"I'm not you." *What a liar you are. You thought about it. You thought about it a lot.*

"That's true. If you were, you'd make darned sure you tied him up first so he didn't go looking somewhere else. If you were me, you'd invite him home with you tonight or you'd go to his place. *I'm* going to Jimmy's again tonight when we both get off work," Liz added. She winked. "I can hardly wait. He's insatiable."

Shawn stood abruptly. "I'd better get back to the table."

"Oh, sit down! We still have five minutes left. I promise I'll quit teasing you. . . ."

But even though their gossip turned to other things, Shawn couldn't stop thinking of the picture Liz had evoked with her talk of Shawn going to bed with Michael. When her break was over, and she went back to the floor, every time she saw him, she remembered, and she wondered what kind of lover he was. What it would be like to make love with him. She was filled with a restless desire that no amount of talking to herself could banish.

She wanted Michael.

It was as simple as that and as complicated as that.

All night long she wondered if he had any idea what she was thinking. All night long she wondered if he felt the same way, if he'd imagined them making love, too.

And all night long she wondered what she'd do if—the next time they were together—he did more than kiss her, if he acted as if he wanted to make love to her.

SIX

Shawn decided to run before going to bed Sunday morning. At nine o'clock, just as she was jogging past Michael's town house unit, his garage door opened. She glanced over, and there was Michael, looking as fresh as if he'd had a full night's sleep—which Shawn knew he hadn't. He'd worked all night the same as she had.

She hesitated, not sure if she should stop or not.

"Shawn," he called. So she stopped, waiting on the sidewalk as he walked slowly down the driveway. He was all dressed up: dark slacks, pale blue shirt, gray sport coat. He removed his dark glasses when he reached her side.

"Good morning," he said, smiling.

Shawn wished his smile weren't so potent. She also wished she were impervious to him. Unfortunately, it was and she wasn't.

Her heart picked up speed, but she kept her voice casual when she answered. Bad enough he affected her this way. She sure as heck didn't want him to know it. "Good morning," she said. "You're up awfully early."

He shrugged. "I wanted to make the nine-thirty folk mass." His toasty eyes glinted in the bright sunshine as he gave her a frankly admiring gaze. "I like the guitars and the kids who sing."

She wondered if he was trying to impress her. God, she was getting paranoid! He'd have had no way of knowing she was going to be running past his house at the exact moment he emerged to go to church.

She was suddenly glad she hadn't thrown on any old pair of shorts and T-shirt the way she usually did. Today she'd worn a new blue outfit and tied her hair back with a matching blue ribbon.

You wore it on purpose, just in case you happened to see Michael. Don't try to pretend otherwise.

"Well, have fun," she said. "I don't want to make you late." She turned to leave.

"Shawn, wait, don't go yet," Michael said.

She stopped.

"Do you have any plans for later today?" he said.

"Actually, yes."

"*All* day?"

"Pretty much." Then she relented. "I haven't gotten any sleep yet, and after I do, I'd planned to paint."

"Could I talk you into going to dinner with me instead?"

"I really shouldn't." She hoped her expression didn't reveal how much she really wanted to say yes.

"You can't work all the time." His voice deepened as his gaze swept her face. "I thought about you all day yesterday," he said softly.

Shawn swallowed. When he looked at her like that,

something went hollow deep inside her. She wet her lips, and his gaze fastened on her mouth. "I . . ." She stopped. Lord have mercy, she was in big trouble if all it took was a look or a smile to make her feel this way.

"How about it?" he coaxed.

Say yes. You want to. "All right."

His eyes brightened with pleasure, and he grinned. "Great! I'll pick you up about seven-thirty, okay?"

She nodded, thinking she had less willpower than a five-year-old who gorges himself on candy and then suffers the consequences.

She should have stood her ground. She should have waited until she heard back from her uncle. She should have at least played hard to get for a while.

Well, too late now. She said good-bye and started off on her run. Michael honked as he passed her a few minutes later, and she waved.

Oh, Shawn, she thought, *you're a mess.*

Pleasure danced in her stomach as she relived the sound of his voice and the look in his eyes when he'd said he'd thought about her ever since Friday night.

Oh, God, she wanted so much to believe that Michael had meant what he'd said, that he wasn't just giving her a line, seeing how easy it would be to add another notch to his belt.

And how are you going to know? What if Philip tells you everything Michael had said is true? What will that prove, anyway? Will it mean you can trust Michael not to let you down? What if you do as Liz has suggested— go to bed with him—and then he drops you?

Shawn's feet pounded the pavement as her thoughts tumbled in confusion.

Her father had never lied to her.

And he'd let her down.

She had trusted him.

He'd betrayed that trust.

Still, as her mother had said, if she never took any chances, how could she know for sure? And her mother had also said she had no regrets.

Shawn hoped whatever happened between her and Michael, she'd be able to say the same thing.

Michael was meeting his godfather for brunch at eleven. Dominic was living in the penthouse suite at the casino, but he'd suggested a restaurant in Henderson, because he didn't want them to meet where anyone might see them.

A few minutes before eleven, Michael parked his Corvette in the parking lot and entered the restaurant. He spotted his godfather immediately, seated at a small table in the corner.

Once Michael was seated, he said, "So how've things been going with you?"

"Good, good," Dominic said. "But let's wait to talk business after we order our food."

A few minutes later, orders placed, cups of coffee in front of them, Dominic said, "I had a call from your father last night."

Michael rolled his eyes. "Doesn't surprise me."

Dominic smiled. "He can't help it, Michael. It's in his nature to want to keep on top of everything. That's why he's been so successful."

"I know, but it gets a little bit tiresome when you're on the receiving end. I can't help feeling he's checking up on me." Michael took a sip of his coffee, grimacing because it was too hot and he'd burned his tongue. "Why can't he just keep his nose out of it, and let me do my job?"

Dominic shrugged. "Victor says you don't think the MacInnes woman is involved."

"No, I don't."

"Are you basing this conclusion on anything other than gut feeling?"

Michael waited until the waitress, who had come with their food, served them. Once she was gone, he picked up his fork and said, "It's pretty much gut feeling. But I have well-honed instincts; you know that." He tasted the cole slaw accompanying his grilled chicken sandwich.

"I know you do," Dominic said slowly. He spread jelly on his toast, having ordered breakfast instead of lunch. He took a bite of his scrambled eggs, then his toast. "But this is too important to rely on instinct alone."

Michael clenched his jaw. Was his godfather going to start lecturing him, too?

"Tell me about her," Dominic said softly.

So Michael did. He finished with, "I think she's pretty much an innocent, in every way."

"Are you dating her?"

"We haven't had what you'd call a date yet, but I'm taking her to dinner tonight." At the thought of the coming evening, Michael felt a warm glow of anticipation. No doubt about it, he was looking forward to spending the evening with Shawn.

"What about the others?" Dominic ate some of his hash browns.

"I've spent a lot of time with Luis Alvarez, because he's the one who's trained me. And I've talked with Jimmy Penner some—not as much as I'd like to, though. I'd really like to spend some time with both of them somewhere other than the casino. I was thinking when I go on the day shift I'd invite Luis to have a drink with me after work.''

"What about Penner?''

"Well, I hear through the grapevine that he's a real basketball nut. I thought maybe I could get some tickets for a UNLV game and invite him to go.''

"Good idea. Want me to take care of it for you?''

"Yes. Only trouble is, how will I explain the tickets? I hear they're nearly impossible to come by.''

Dominic thought for a minute while he polished off his eggs. Then he grinned. "Why not say you won them in a poker game?''

Michael smiled slowly. "I like it.''

"What about Hazlett, O'Brien, and Ford?'' Dominic asked, naming the other three floormen who had been at The Glass Slipper long enough to be considered suspects.

"I've got a date to play golf with Floyd Hazlett and Walker Ford next weekend. As for Danny O'Brien . . . well, I haven't made any inroads with him yet. I haven't had much of an opportunity.'' He stopped talking as their waitress approached and refilled their coffee cups.

When she left he said, "You know, I've been doing a lot of thinking. Why don't we install a camera in the counting room of the cashier's office?''

Michael was referring to the room where all the money brought in from the floor was counted before being deposited in the casino accounts.

"It seems to me,'' Michael continued before his godfather could comment on his suggestion, "that during the counting, the casino is the most vulnerable to theft.''

"But three people are involved in the counting. And

they're not always the same three people," Dominic pointed out.

"True, but the same three people are usually involved in any one shift."

Dominic nodded slowly. "You're right." Then he frowned. "But why didn't our auditors pick up some kind of pattern, then?"

"How could they?" Michael said. "I checked. They only looked at daily income totals—not shift totals."

"You know, Michael, you may have something here!" Dominic said, excitement firing his dark eyes. "But wait a minute. . . . How could we install a camera without anyone knowing about it? The cashier's office always has people in it, twenty-four hours a day."

"Well, I thought about that, too," Michael said. He drank some of his coffee. "What if we started painting all the offices? They need it, and we planned to give the whole place a face-lift, anyway. That way, when that particular room was done, no one would think anything of a couple of men being in there working."

"You know, Michael, that's a great idea. Have you mentioned this to Victor?"

"Not yet."

"I'm going to talk to him tonight. Do you want me to bounce it off him?"

"Sure."

"I'm certain he'll like it." Dominic gave him an approving look. "You're doing good work, Michael."

Michael rubbed his forehead. "Thanks. But you know, I really hate this."

Dominic's dark eyes were sympathetic. "I know you do. Hell, we all do."

Michael pushed his plate away. Now was the time

he wished he had a cigarette, but he'd given them up five years ago. "This is more than just not liking the situation, Uncle Dominic. I'm completely burned out on this kind of thing. I just want to live like any other ordinary person lives—no lies, no sneaking around, no ulterior motives. If I like someone, I want to be able to spend time with them, and I don't want to spy on them."

"This'll soon be over," Dominic said soothingly. "And maybe we'll be lucky. Maybe we'll find our crook with this hidden camera."

"I hope so. I can't wait to get out of this place." Yet Michael knew he wasn't being completely honest with his godfather. He couldn't wait until this investigation was over, that was true enough, but he wasn't completely unhappy about being in Las Vegas.

Not since meeting Shawn.

Shawn.

He thought about how she'd looked this morning when he'd seen her as he was leaving for mass at St. Ann's. With her bright hair tied up, her creamy skin devoid of makeup, and her shorts and T-shirt on, she'd looked like a teenager. An innocent, sweet young girl.

But she's not a young girl, is she? She's a woman. A very desirable woman. And the feelings she causes in you are decidedly adult feelings.

For the rest of his meal with his godfather, Michael tried to put Shawn out of his mind and concentrate on what Dominic had to say. But later, as he drove back to the city, he allowed himself to think of her again.

In only a few hours he would see her. He wondered how she would act. He wondered if she'd let him kiss her again. He wanted to do much more than kiss her, and if this were an ordinary date, if he had no ulterior motive in asking her out, he would probably act on his desires. He would probably try to make love to her.

But this wasn't an ordinary date, and no amount of wishing would make it so. He was in Las Vegas for a reason, and Shawn MacInnes was part of that reason. Regret coursed through him. No matter how much he wanted to, he'd better not make love to Shawn tonight.

"Shawn, will you stop fidgeting?" Annika said. "I'm going to smear your polish!"

"Sorry." Shawn tried to sit still while Annika finished the manicure.

"That's the problem with not dating much. You get all uptight when you *do* have a date," Annika said, smiling good-naturedly. "Now, sit still. I'm almost finished." She carefully polished the last nail on Shawn's hand. "There! Now wave them around for a few minutes, then I'll put a top coat on."

"I don't know why you're making such a big deal out of this. I'm only going out to dinner with the man." But Shawn waved her hands around obediently.

Annika leaned back in her chair, her green eyes sparkling in the bright kitchen. The late afternoon sunlight streamed through the window, backlighting her hair with a scarlet halo. "Don't play games with me, Shawn. I've lived with you for a year, remember? You really *like* this guy."

For at least the millionth time, Shawn wished she looked like Annika. "Am I that transparent?"

Annika shrugged.

"Liz says I should grab him. Make sure no one else gets her hooks into him."

"That's just common sense," Annika said. "Eligible men don't grow on trees, you know."

She knew. "Liz also said I should go to bed with him." Shawn met Annika's gaze. "What do you think? Would you have sex with a man you'd only known a week?"

"Depends on the man," Annika said without hesitation.

"Don't you think a person should be in love before making love?"

"Not necessarily. There's nothing wrong with taking your pleasure, as long as you're honest about it. If one person's in love, and the other person pretends to be but isn't, well, I think *that's* wrong." Annika began applying the top coat to Shawn's fingernails. "Jeez, why shouldn't a woman enjoy herself? Men do it all the time!"

Shawn nodded. "I know. Maybe that's what bothers me."

"Are you thinking about making love with Michael?"

"I guess I am."

"Did he want to the other night?"

"No."

Annika's eyes glinted. "But he must have done *something* to get you started thinking in this direction."

"He kissed me. That's all." Her face felt warm. Even though she was the one who had initiated this conversation because she really wanted to know what Annika thought, she still felt uncomfortable discussing something so personal. She wondered if she'd ever feel comfortable when the subject was sex. "But I have a feeling tonight he may want more."

"Well, hon, the best advice I can give you—give me your other hand—is to just go with the flow." Annika stopped polishing for a moment, her green gaze meeting Shawn's. "See how you feel at the time. If he kisses you, and tries to take it further, and you want him to . . . just do it. And if you don't, say no."

Shawn nodded slowly.

Just do it.

Just say no.

Annika made it all sound so easy.

"Relax. You'll be okay. Trust me," Annika said. "Now, do you want me to give you a pedicure, too?"

Shawn looked at her blankly. "Well, that's going a little far, don't you think?"

"I don't know. . . . I mean, if you're thinking about making love tonight, you'll want everything to look good, won't you? Who knows? Your Michael may have a foot fetish." Annika was obviously fighting a grin. "I've heard about these guys who like to suck on toes . . . so you'd better be prepared. . . ." She lost her battle and started to giggle, laughing harder as Shawn reached into the little bowl they kept in the center of the table, took out a toothpick, and threw it at her.

"If you're finished, I've got to go get ready," Shawn said dryly.

As she climbed the stairs to her bedroom, Annika called out, "Do you want to borrow my black satin tap pants and matching bra?"

Shawn refused to answer.

An hour later, as Shawn came back downstairs to wait for Michael's arrival, she was still thinking about Annika's teasing suggestions. For some reason, she couldn't get the picture of Michael and her toes out of her mind.

What was wrong with her? she wondered. She certainly didn't *want* to do anything kinky. And what Annika had suggested was definitely kinky. So why couldn't she forget about it?

Suddenly, out of nowhere, a long-forgotten memory assailed her. She'd been ten years old, in the fourth grade, and one of the little boys in her class had whispered the "F" word to her. It was the first time she'd ever heard the word, and that night, she'd asked her father about it.

Gerald had explained that it was a nasty word, and she should just forget she'd ever heard it. "But if that little so-and-so ever says it to you again, you tell him you're going to have your father call his father," Gerald added.

Wide-eyed, Shawn nodded. But later, when she was in bed, she kept thinking of the word. And that Sunday, during Sunday school class, she kept wanting to say the word out loud. She knew it was a bad word. She knew her Sunday school teacher, Miss MacAllister, would be horrified if Shawn were to say the word. Still she wanted to. And she was ashamed of herself. She knew if her mother or father or Miss MacAllister knew what she was thinking, they wouldn't like her anymore.

Shawn had forgotten that long-ago episode. Her one tiny act of rebellion in a life spent doing the right thing.

Oh, so big deal! So you're thinking about something just a little bit naughty. So what?

She sighed, wishing Annika hadn't planted that titillating picture in her mind, because she knew darned well that off and on throughout the evening, she would think about it, and even if it *was* harmless, she didn't want to think about it. She wanted—needed—all her wits about her tonight. Her attraction to Michael was potent enough. It didn't need any added enhancements or temptations.

She glanced at the clock on the mantel. Almost seven-thirty. Michael would arrive at any moment. Sure enough, just as the thought crossed her mind, the doorbell rang. She stood, smoothing down the skirt of her teal dress. She hadn't been sure how dressed up she should get, but finally decided on a dress and matching flats. Dressy enough to go anywhere, and not too dressy if Michael chose a casual place.

She slowly walked to the door.

Michael knew he was in trouble the minute Shawn opened the door. He took one look at her, and all his good resolutions flew out the window.

She looked beautiful.

The shade of green she was wearing made her hair and eyes and skin look even better than they had looked the other night.

He couldn't believe how she affected him. Michael was not inexperienced. He had dated many women over the years, most of them much more sophisticated than Shawn, many of them even more beautiful. But there was something about Shawn that none of those other women had possessed, and he had noticed it the very first time he'd set eyes on her.

As she smiled up at him shyly, old-fashioned words like purity and goodness kept coming to mind. *Jesus, Vellini, this woman has got you completely bamboozled.*

"Hi," she said. "I'm ready. Let me just get my jacket, okay?"

"Sure." He walked into the foyer while she disappeared into the living room. A few seconds later, she was back, a black jacket folded over her arm.

Soon they were settled into his car, and as they drove

out of the complex, Michael thought how much he liked having Shawn here beside him.

"Where are we going?" she asked after a moment.

"Do you like Italian food?"

"I love it."

"Well, how about Mama Angela's?" He glanced over at her. "One of the guys recommended it."

"That's one of my favorite places to eat."

"Good."

As they drove toward the city, Michael wished once more that this were just an ordinary date.

But nothing about his relationship with Shawn could ever be ordinary, because there was nothing ordinary about her.

Or about his feelings for her.

Michael suddenly had a sinking feeling in his stomach.

What in God's name would he do if he was wrong about her? Could he turn her over to the authorities if he found out she was mixed up in the skimming operation?

Why couldn't Shawn have been the kind of woman he'd imagined her to be before meeting her? That would have made things so much more simple.

But even if Shawn was innocent as he believed her to be, he knew there was no way things could ever work out between them, even if he wanted them to. Because even if he was right about Shawn, how was she going to feel when she found out he'd been lying to her?

She'll hate you. She'll never want to see you again.

The knowledge hammered at him. All the way to the restaurant he kept thinking about it. The thought of Shawn hating him filled him with a deep regret and something else. Something very like pain.

_____ SEVEN _____

Shawn knew she'd never remember everything she and Michael talked about during dinner. She was too aware of him on a physical and emotional level, and everything about Mama Angela's conspired to enhance the sensory experience of the evening.

First there were the smells: garlic and tomatoes and onions and the aroma of freshly baked bread and pizza dough.

Then there were the sights: the bright red and white checkered tablecloths, the flickering candles in old Chianti bottles, the framed pictures of Venice and Florence and Rome and Milan, and the proudly displayed photographs of Mama's family. Lastly, there were the sounds: people talking and laughing, dishes clinking, the members of Mama's family calling orders, and the lively music emanating from the accordion player, who strolled between the tables.

But one conversation stood out, because it concerned her father.

"This is a great place," Michael said as he sampled some of the antipasto salad that was the restaurant's trademark.

Shawn smiled. "Yes, I've always loved it."

"Do you come here often?" Michael lifted the napkin covering the hot garlic bread and took a crusty wedge.

"My parents used to come here all the time, and they always brought me." Sadness threatened as thoughts of those happy days flickered through her mind, and she fought to banish it. This was not a night to remember the past, she told herself. This was a night to contemplate the future.

"You loved your father an awful lot," Michael said, his eyes serious as he watched her face.

Shawn nodded wordlessly. Darn it! Why did the memories of her father continue to haunt her? Continue to hurt her? And why did she always show her feelings so openly?

Michael seemed about to say something else, then hesitated. "It's none of my business," he finally said slowly, laying his fork down, "but it's been a long time since he died . . . yet you still seem to be grieving."

Shawn looked down at her plate of salad. The noises of the restaurant faded, and now there was only Michael's low voice. He was entirely too perceptive.

She knew what he was trying to say. It was time to get on with her life, to put the old hurts behind her. Essentially he was saying the same things her mother had said the other day. Shawn marshaled what inner strength she had, lifted her head, and faced Michael's compassionate gaze. "You think I'm dwelling on the past."

He shrugged. "I don't have any right to tell you how

to live your life, but I do understand, more than most people would. Remember, I've got a similar situation. I lost my mother, a lot more recently than you lost your father. And it hurt. But I try not to focus on the sadness of losing her. I try to remember the good times instead.''

"But your mother didn't kill herself," Shawn said, hearing the bitterness in her voice yet unable to banish it. "Your mother didn't deliberately leave you. She left because she had no choice. My father had a choice. And he chose to desert me and my mother." Shawn drew a shaky breath. "That's what I can't forget. Or forgive."

"Do you want to?"

Shawn's startled gaze met his steady one. The quiet question rocked her. *Did* she want to? Or was she clinging to her pain? Blaming her father for her inability to build other relationships? For her fear of committing herself?

Stunned, Shawn didn't answer. The accordion player, one of Mama Angela's cousins, approached their table, his rousing rendition of "Three Coins in the Fountain" grating on her tense nerves.

Michael said something to him, and the accordion player nodded in understanding and wandered off.

Shawn stared at Michael. Her heart beat in heavy thumps against her chest as she absorbed his words.

Was Michael right? Did she hide behind the desertion and betrayal of her father? Use it as a reason to avoid strong emotions? Was that why she had shied away from relationships with men? Was her rationale about not getting involved with anyone who worked in the gambling industry really a smoke screen to hide from her *real* fears?

After a few tense moments, Michael reached across the table and covered her right hand with his. The feel of his warm palm against hers was comforting. "Shawn, I'm no psychologist, and you can tell me to shut up if I'm out of line, but it seems to me that anyone who commits suicide has serious problems and is probably clinically depressed. I've read a little about survivors of suicides, and how they always feel abandoned and betrayed, and according to the experts, your feelings aren't unusual. But they *are* destructive."

As Shawn absorbed Michael's words and the warmth of contact between them, she wondered again at the understanding and intelligence behind them.

Surely a man with his sensitivity was honest.

Surely she could trust him.

She chewed on her bottom lip, then sighed deeply. "I know you're right. My mother said something very similar the other day."

Michael smiled softly, squeezed her hand, then let it go. "Eat your salad," he said kindly. "And I'll tell you a little story."

Shawn lifted her fork and began to eat.

"Ever since my mother died, my father's been a different person. All his less than admirable qualities have been emphasized. For the past few years, I've really had to fight to keep him from controlling my life. I'm still fighting, and it's tough sometimes, because I love him, but I know I need to get away from him. I need to build my own life."

"But I *have* built my own life," Shawn said. "I support myself. I live alone. My mother doesn't tell me what to do or how to do it."

"Well, yes, you're right. But there *are* similarities

between our situations, similarities that aren't that obvious on the surface of things.''

"You think so?"

Michael finished the last forkful of his salad and wiped his mouth with his napkin. "I do. I think both of us are still shackled by who we are in relation to our fathers. We need to be who we are without restraints.'' He smiled ruefully. "I don't even know if that makes sense, but *I* understand what I mean.''

For the first time since the conversation about her father had started, Shawn smiled. Her gaze met Michael's. "I think I do, too. And . . . I think you just might be right.''

"Good.''

His smile made his eyes light up, and Shawn thought about how important Michael had become to her in just a few short days. She wondered at the turn of fate that had made her go to breakfast with him that first morning.

"Now let's eat a lot and drink a little of this wine— not too much, because we have to go to work later tonight—and forget all about anything serious. Okay?'' he said.

"It's a deal.''

Later, as they drove home, Shawn kept remembering Michael's revelations about his father as well as his advice. Something he hadn't said—maybe because he didn't know her well enough to realize it—was that Shawn, in addition to letting go of the past, needed to let go of some of her inhibitions and fears in other areas.

Take a few chances, as her mother had said.

Live it up, as Liz would say.

Go with the flow, as Annika had counseled.

Should she? she wondered. Should she do as they'd all suggested? Maybe tonight?

Once more the erotic image of bare toes and Michael danced through her mind.

She hardly noticed the desert landscape as it flew by—the Joshua trees dotting the road, the yucca plants, and the inky outline of the mountains in the distance.

As Michael's Corvette sped through the silvery moonlit night, and a Paula Abdul disc played softly on the CD player, the only thing Shawn was completely aware of was Michael.

And over and over, through her mind, the same question tumbled.

Should she let Michael know she wanted him to make love to her?

Because she already knew Michael well enough to realize he was not the kind of man to force the issue. He would ask, he might even try to persuade her, but he would never force her.

The decision was hers.

Michael kept telling himself, over and over again, that no matter how he felt, he must not make love to Shawn. Ironically, the more he was around her, the more he wanted to deepen their relationship. Yet, conversely, the more he was around her, the more he realized that Shawn was not a woman he could make love to casually, then walk away from.

First of all, if he did that, he would hate himself.

Secondly, he would hurt her deeply.

And Shawn had been hurt enough.

Although he'd advised her to get on with her life, he knew her emotions were fragile. It would take a long time for her to come to terms with her father's abandonment, and if she were to be abandoned by someone else she loved, it might be catastrophic.

And Michael knew, with a certainty that came from deep within, that if Shawn were to give herself to him, it would be because she was already halfway in love with him.

He couldn't make love to her unless he knew he loved her, too. He couldn't betray her in that way.

But you're willing to betray her in other ways, aren't you?

The relentless voice of his conscience wouldn't leave him alone tonight.

Michael sighed, cutting a glance at Shawn's profile. Her vulnerability tore at his heart in a way no woman had ever managed to touch him. No one was more surprised by this than he was. As he watched her, she sighed softly, and something deep within him stirred in response. At that moment, all he wanted was to take care of Shawn, to wipe the sadness he'd seen earlier out of her eyes, to make her laugh, to keep her safe and happy.

He looked away abruptly and stared at the moonlit road. Slowly a certainty spread through him. A certainty that made his mouth go dry and his breath catch. The knowledge thrummed within in time to the sound of the Corvette's tires against the road.

The worst possible thing that could happen was happening. He was falling in love with her. There was no way he could remain objective any longer. If he had any scruples at all, he would tell his father at once. He would remove himself from the investigation.

He swore softly, damning himself, damning his father. He was in a hell of a mess.

A mess he saw no way out of. For if he did that, if

he leveled with his father, he would lose Shawn before he'd ever had a chance to know if they had any kind of future together.

And no matter what he'd told his father or his godfather, the fact remained that he wasn't completely sure Shawn was innocent.

Perhaps he was falling in love with a thief.

A very clever, very lovely, very accomplished thief.

By the time they reached their town home complex, Shawn had made up her mind. No matter how much she might want to, it was too soon to make love with Michael. Whether her friends made fun of her or not.

She had to remain true to herself, and she simply didn't know him well enough yet. She didn't know her own feelings about him well enough yet.

She felt better for making the decision. She hoped he would understand.

You ninny. He may not even try to make love to you. For that matter, he may not even kiss you. In fact, he may be thoroughly sick of you and think of you as a sad-eyed whiner, after that scene in the restaurant tonight.

As he turned onto their street, he said, "It's only ten o'clock. Would you like to come to my place for some coffee?"

She shouldn't.

"I've got some French roast. Do you like French roast?"

On the other hand, if she didn't go to his place, he would probably expect to be invited into hers. And how much could happen in an hour or so? By eleven they would need to get ready for work. Besides, if she was considering having sex with Michael, even in the distant future, she needed to spend as much time as possible with him.

"All right."

They entered the town home through the garage, and Shawn was startled to see that Michael's unit had an elaborate security system.

"Did you have that installed?" she asked as she watched him punch in a code.

He nodded.

Fleetingly Shawn wondered why Michael had felt the need for the extra security of an indoor alarm system when the entire complex was noted for its security.

"Go on into the living room and make yourself comfortable," Michael said, "while I get the coffee on."

The moment Shawn entered the L-shaped living area, she knew she and Michael shared more than the loss of a parent, more than the wish to devote themselves to the businesses they loved, and more than a potent sexual attraction. They obviously shared a love of color and had similar tastes in furnishings.

She looked around in admiration. Like her unit, the living area had huge expanses of window and was open and airy-looking. Michael had furnished it with an enormous sectional sofa covered with a nubby fabric of pale sea green and oatmeal, with touches of a deeper jade running through it. He'd accented the colors in the couch with a navy blue chair and throw pillows.

His coffee table was glass with a light oak pedestal. Everywhere she looked she saw beautiful things: Wedgewood boxes, crystal sculptures, elegant paperweights. There was expensive-looking stereo equipment and a state-of-the art big-screen TV. Nowhere did she see spartan living or self-denial. She was beginning to understand the extra security measures. These furnishings represented a lot of money.

Shawn wandered slowly around, looking at the paintings on the walls. Most were signed prints, but there were a couple of originals by names she recognized. Names she admired, like Georgia O'Keefe.

Why hadn't Michael mentioned that he was an art buff? She frowned, thinking back to their conversations about her painting. He'd never indicated he had any more than a cursory knowledge of art.

A small oil, painted in vibrant yet soft colors and lighted from above, caught her eye. She walked slowly over and studied it. It was an exquisitely rendered painting of two young girls sitting on a park bench. Suddenly Shawn gasped. The painting was an original Monet. She would stake her life on it.

"Do you like the Monet?" Michael said as he walked up behind her.

Shawn didn't turn around. She was still stunned by her discovery and still trying to figure out what it meant. "It's breathtaking. I suppose this is another gift from your father?" She knew her tone was slightly belligerent, but her mind was whirling with questions. Just what was going on here? How in the world could his father afford to gift Michael with a Monet? If he had *that* much money, why should Michael sweat start-up costs for his restaurant?

"No," he said quietly, "that painting belonged to my mother. She gave it to me right before she died, because she knew I loved it."

Slowly she turned around. She searched his face. Was he telling her the truth? Obviously Michael DeNiro had grown up a child of privilege—well educated and sophisticated—accustomed to the best. "No wonder you have that elaborate security system. Paintings like this one are normally only seen in museums. It must be worth a fortune."

Michael shrugged. "I suppose it is. I haven't had it appraised in a while."

How much of what he said could she believe? Maybe his professed desire to open a restaurant was just a lot of guff. Maybe he'd just said that to make her think they had something in common. Maybe everything he'd told her was designed to soften her up. Maybe all he wanted was to get her into bed, then brag about his conquest. Shawn knew the guys at the casino—guys like Luis—talked about her all the time. That she'd become some kind of challenge to them. Perhaps Michael was really just like them after all.

Her face must have reflected her feelings, because Michael put his hands on her shoulders. "Shawn, what's wrong?"

"Michael, I simply don't know what to believe anymore."

He frowned, his eyes darkening. "What do you mean?"

Shawn took a deep breath. "Michael, if I ask you a question, will you tell me the truth?"

For the briefest moment, something flickered in the depths of his eyes. Quickly hidden, but there nevertheless.

Something inside Shawn withered. Even as Michael said, "Of course I'll tell you the truth," she knew down deep that maybe he would, and maybe he wouldn't.

She wasn't sure why, or how, but the certainty grew within her that Michael DeNiro was a very complicated man who was hiding something from her.

What was it?

"Who are you, Michael?" she whispered. "Just who are you?"

Michael knew he'd blown it. Somehow, in some way, he'd given something away. He'd let her know he hadn't been entirely truthful with her.

At that moment, looking down at the suspicion shining in Shawn's blue eyes, if he'd had his father there, he'd have strangled him—cheerfully, and without remorse.

Think fast, buddy-boy. Say something.

"Who am I?" he repeated, playing for time. "What do you mean?"

Her eyes narrowed, and the vulnerability he associated with her disappeared, to be replaced with a stubborn tilt to her chin and a strong determination in her steely look. "Just what I said. Who are you?"

He sighed. "I'm exactly who I said I am—a man trying to break away from his father's shadow. A father who is very wealthy and very powerful and used to getting his own way. A father who is not above bribes to keep his son on the straight and narrow."

And if she didn't believe him, there wasn't much he could do about it, because what he'd just told her was the simple truth. He'd told her the truth about the Monet, too. He could only hope that she believed him.

He could see her assimilating his answer, sifting through it, looking for weaknesses, looking for lies.

After what seemed like a very long time, her expression softened. She shook her head. "Maybe I'm a stupid fool, but God help me, I believe you."

Michael expelled his breath. He smiled, looking deep into her eyes. He wished with all his heart he could tell her the rest. Tell her everything and beg her to forgive him for deceiving her.

His hands on her arms tightened, and suddenly the expression in her eyes changed. Warmed. Awareness sizzled between them, the very air heavy with it. He could see the pulse in her throat beating, and with each breath she took, her breasts rose and fell. It was very quiet in the room. From the kitchen he could hear the faint gurgle of the coffee maker, and from the fireplace, the ticking of the clock mounted above it.

So many thoughts whirled through Michael's head. So many regrets. So many desires.

He knew he should back away. Go get the coffee. Stop touching her.

He couldn't.

The moment seemed suspended in time as their gazes locked.

Just as he thought he could stand the tension no longer, she whispered, "Michael, kiss me."

His kiss was everything she'd remembered and more. It was heat and desire and passion and a wild kind of joy. It was her heart pounding against her chest and her blood rushing through her veins. It was fireworks and bells and a crazy kaleidoscope of sensation. It was everything she'd ever read about or thought about or wanted.

It was Michael. The taste of him, exciting and strong and so wonderfully male. The smell of him, a combination of scents both familiar and erotic. The feel of him: his hair, thick and springy under her fingers and his hands as they molded her back and slid to her bottom, pulling her closer so that she could feel his arousal.

As Shawn lost herself in the delicious torment of his

kiss, she deliberately shoved aside all her fears and questions. She stopped thinking, stopped worrying, and just let herself feel.

Go with the flow.

And she went with it. She opened her mouth under his and met his tongue thrust for thrust. She absorbed him, inhaled him, and put everything she was and everything she hoped to be in her response.

The kiss went on and on.

Became two kisses, then three.

Soon all there was in the entire universe was a maelstrom of sensation, the feeling that she'd been caught up in forces over which she had no control.

As Michael's mouth slid to her throat, she arched her back. His hands moved up her rib cage until their warmth covered her breasts. Shawn moaned softly as he caressed her. She could feel the heat inside her building with each passing moment. Her heart thundered in her chest as his lips captured her in another deep, drugging kiss.

"Shawn, Shawn," he muttered against her mouth as he finally broke the kiss. "If we don't stop now, I'm not going to be able to." Breathing raggedly and obviously struggling for control, he reached up to remove her hands from his neck.

Everything in Shawn cried out in protest. She wanted more. Now that she'd let herself go, she didn't want to stop. She didn't want to think, either. She just wanted to feel.

She wanted him to love her.

Now. Tonight. Right here.

She wanted to experience everything there was to experience with him. She wanted to know the secret everyone else seemed to know and which had evaded her for so long.

So she resisted his efforts to pull away. Instead, she locked her arms around his neck and pulled his head down, whispering, "Michael . . . don't talk . . . just . . . just make love to me. . . ."

He stiffened, looking deeply into her eyes, his own eyes troubled. "Shawn, are you sure? God knows, I want to, but are you sure this is what *you* really want?"

"Yes," she said, but his question disturbed her. "I . . . I'm sure." Didn't *he* want to?

"Shawn . . ." He frowned, shaking his head. "You don't sound sure to me. I . . . I think we should wait."

Oh, God, Shawn thought. *What have I done?* Embarrassment and shame welled together in her throat, and she couldn't meet his gaze.

Michael didn't want to make love to her.

She'd asked him to kiss her, and he'd obliged, but he didn't want it to go any further.

Now he was trying to let her down gently.

Mortified, she didn't know what to do or where to look.

"Shawn, don't look like that."

"I . . . It's okay, Michael," she mumbled. *Where was her purse? She had to get out of here.* "You don't have to explain. I understand."

"Jesus, Shawn, I don't think you do!"

Shawn looked around wildly. Where had she put her stupid purse? She moved toward the couch.

"Shawn—" He reached for her arm.

"Let me go, Michael," she said, still not looking at him. "I'd like to leave now, if you don't mind."

"Damn it, Shawn, would you please look at me? Would you at least *listen*? You've got to understand. I want you. In fact, I want you more than I've ever wanted any woman. I want you so badly, I hurt. But I want you to be sure. If we make love, I don't want you to have any regrets afterward.''

She nodded. Anything to get out of here. She could feel the tears at the back of her eyes. That's all she needed to do to complete her humiliation. Cry in front of him.

"Shawn, please . . ."

"It's okay, Michael, really it is. Don't give it another thought." She finally spied her purse, sitting on top of the stereo cabinet. Almost sobbing with relief, she rushed over, scooped it up, and headed for the foyer. She could hear him behind her. *Quick, quick. Open the door. Get out.*

The cool night air rushed in as she yanked open the front door. "Good night, Michael. Thanks for the dinner. I'll see you at work."

"Shawn, dammit, look at me."

She stopped. She had no choice. He had grabbed her hand and wouldn't let go. Rather than humiliate herself further by causing a scene, she turned. Fighting back the tears she knew were lurking somewhere very close to the surface, she lifted her head. *Don't let him see you care.*

"Oh, Shawn . . ." Still holding her hand, he brushed her cheek with his other hand, causing quicksilver to flood her veins. He bent down and kissed her mouth very gently, running the tip of his tongue across her lower lip. Then he pulled her into his arms, cradling her head against his chest. He kissed the top of her head, then murmured, "We'll talk about this tomorrow night, after you've had a chance to think. I'll call you, okay?"

She nodded, her emotions chaotic. The only thing she was sure of was that she had to get away.

A few seconds later he released her. But he insisted on walking home with her and stood outside her unit, watching, until she was safely inside.

When the door closed behind her, Shawn leaned against it and closed her eyes. Now the tears that she'd suppressed slid down her cheeks in slow, hot rivulets of humiliation.

He'd said he'd call her.

He wouldn't call her.

She'd made a total fool of herself. She was stupid, stupid. She'd practically thrown herself at him, and because Michael was obviously well brought up and a gentleman, he'd tried to let her down as gently as possible.

But no matter what Michael had said and done, one thing stood out clearly.

She'd offered herself to him, and he'd rejected her.

Damn it to hell! How had everything gotten so complicated? The last thing he'd wanted to do was hurt Shawn, and he'd done just that. It was obvious she'd felt rejected and thought he didn't want to make love to her.

Jesus, if she only knew. It had taken every bit of his willpower to pull away from her. He'd wanted her so badly, he'd just about burst with it.

He'd tried to be noble, tried to do the right thing, and it had backfired.

Oh, Shawn, why is life so difficult sometimes?

He felt like a complete heel.

Sighing, he walked home and began to get ready for work. As he changed into his uniform, he thought about how quickly things changed; how quickly things seemed to escalate out of his control, no matter what he originally planned.

He grimaced as he tied his black bow tie. Until this assignment, he'd always prided himself on how ordered his life was. No more. A certain redhead had taken care of that.

He looked at his watch. Almost eleven-thirty. Time to leave for the casino. He had intended to ask Shawn if she wanted to ride to work with him. Now, though, he knew it would be much better to leave her alone.

But only until tomorrow, he decided. Tomorrow he would have to repair the damage he'd caused tonight. Michael sighed wearily. It sounded easier than it would be, he knew. He wasn't sure if he *could* repair the damage.

EIGHT

Shawn jumped every time the phone rang. She was afraid each caller might be Michael. And then when it wasn't, she felt both relieved and disappointed at the same time.

What a mess you are! You can't even decide how you feel, let alone what to do about it.

She put down her paintbrush and stood. Stretching her tired muscles, she studied the painting on her drawing table. Her work was not going well today. And it was no wonder, she thought, when her mind had been on one thing and one thing only: Michael.

Desultorily she walked toward the window, parted the curtains, and looked down at the street. By craning her neck, she could just see the sidewalk and driveway of Michael's unit.

She knew he'd call her eventually. Oh, God. What was she going to do?

She stared unseeing out the window. Tears filled her eyes, and she felt like screaming. What was *wrong* with her? The past sixteen hours had been the most miserable of her life. No, that wasn't quite true. She'd been more miserable after her father had died, but this was pretty bad. On a misery scale it ranked right up there at about a nine.

Last night, after she'd left Michael's place in such a rush, she knew there was no way, absolutely no way, she could face him at work. So she'd done something she rarely did: She called in sick. She didn't even feel guilty. She *was* sick. Heartsick.

But she couldn't hide out forever.

She'd have to face him sometime.

She'd have to talk to him sometime.

Shawn let the curtain fall back. Listlessly she contemplated her half-finished painting—a project she'd been looking forward to for a long time.

Weeks ago, on one of those rare, overcast days that Las Vegas seldom saw, Shawn had wheedled Annika into posing for her. Wearing a white satin nightgown that molded to her body, Annika stood against the backdrop of the tall yucca plant in their backyard. She had reminded Shawn of a young goddess, with her head thrown back, her chest jutting out, and a dreamy look on her face.

Paying no attention to Annika's frequent grumbling, Shawn shot two rolls of film. She'd known the planned painting could be one of her best, and a thrill of excitement shot through her as she anticipated working on it.

She had started it yesterday, but because she'd been so preoccupied with thoughts of Michael, she was less than satisfied with its progress. Instead of stylistic, the painting looked pretentious. Instead of pensive, Annika looked petulant. Shawn knew the fault was hers. After all, the photos as well as the concept were great.

Come on! Buck up. Quit thinking about last night and Michael. What's done is done and can't be changed. So you made a fool of yourself. So what? It's not the end of the world. You'll be out of this town by next spring, and you'll never have to see Michael DeNiro again.

Disgusted with herself, Shawn decided to make something to eat. When she worked the night shift, she rarely ate any breakfast. Somehow breakfast at one or two o'clock in the afternoon didn't appeal to her. She headed toward the kitchen while making a mental inventory of the refrigerator and pantry. Tuna fish sounded good, she thought.

She had no sooner removed a can of tuna from the pantry when the phone rang.

She froze, staring at the extension mounted on the kitchen wall.

Michael.

What was she going to say to him? What did a person say when she'd thrown herself at a man, and he'd rejected her? Oh, he'd *said* he wanted her, he'd *said* he just wanted her to be sure, but he had obviously been trying to let her down gently. He'd *thought* he was interested in her, then for some reason, he'd changed his mind. After all, she'd been the one to ask him to kiss her.

On and on her mind whirled as, slowly, she walked toward the phone. She picked it up. "Hello?"

"Shawn?"

Her heart started beating double time. It *was* Michael. "Hello, Michael," she said. *Be cool. Be distant. You could care less that he called you. You hardly remember last night.*

"Are you busy?" he asked.

"Just fixing myself a sandwich."

"Oh."

He sounds nervous.

"Uh . . . I was thinking. Would you like to come over here tonight?"

Shawn's heart raced.

"Shawn?" He sounded tentative and unsure of himself.

She sighed. "I heard you, Michael."

"I thought I could order a pizza. We could talk."

"I don't know if that's such a good idea. Maybe we should just forget—"

"I can't forget what happened last night. I've thought of nothing but you since you left."

Shawn's stomach twisted. She closed her eyes.

His voice dropped to a soft murmur. "Shawn, I have to see you. We can't leave things this way."

"I don't know," she whispered.

What should she do? She was scared now. If they'd made love last night, before she'd really had a chance to think about what she was doing, that would have been different. But now, after a long night and a longer day, she *had* been thinking. And somehow she knew, without him saying so, that if she went over there tonight, they *would* make love.

And then what? She knew she was falling in love with Michael. But what if, after making love, he decided she wasn't his type at all? What if she disappointed him and he completely lost interest? Could she handle that?

Could she handle another rejection?

Just do it.

Go with the flow.

Take a chance.

If you never gamble, you'll never know what might have happened.

Her heart was pounding so hard, she was sure Michael could hear it through the phone wires.

"What time did you want me to come?" she asked.

Shawn's nerves were so close to the surface, the slightest sound felt like chalk grating against a chalkboard. By the time six o'clock rolled around—the agreed-upon time for her to go over to Michael's—she was a mess.

With butterflies dancing around in her stomach, she did some deep-breathing exercises to calm herself. She was grateful for one thing, though. Annika wasn't home today. She'd spent last night at Darryl's, and since Monday nights were dark at her showroom, she would probably just stay there tonight as well. Shawn wasn't sure she could have withstood Annika's knowing eyes and teasing comments tonight.

Before walking out the door, Shawn decided to check herself out in the mirror one last time. She walked slowly over to the floor-to-ceiling mirror that graced one end of their dining alcove and studied herself.

Sighing, she thought she looked as good as she could look, considering what she had to work with. She had agonized over what to wear tonight. She didn't want to look too schoolteacherish and prim, as she had been accused of looking many times by Annika and Liz. Nor did she want to wear something too suggestive. She laughed at herself. She really didn't own anything suggestive.

She'd finally settled on her favorite outfit, soft peach wool tailored slacks with a matching silky blouse. She checked everything else off on her mental checklist:

contact lenses instead of her glasses, her hair loose and
brushed until it shone, simple gold hoop earrings, taupe
flats, her dark green cardigan sweater, her makeup the
way Annika had shown her. . . . She was ready.

As ready as I'll ever be, anyway.

"Okay, Michael," she whispered. "Here goes nothing." She picked up her purse, opened the front door,
and took a deep, shaky breath. "Or everything . . ."

Two minutes later she pressed Michael's doorbell.
The butterflies were no longer dancing. Now they felt
as if they were having a war in her stomach.

*Oh, what am I doing? Maybe I should just turn
around and run in the other direction!*

The door opened. A smiling Michael stood inside.
"Hi," he said, his eyes filled with a welcoming light.

Shawn's knees suddenly felt unsteady. "Hi."

He stood aside. "Come on in."

She didn't meet his eyes as she brushed past him.
Doubts assailed her from all directions.

She must be crazy.

She'd only known this man a week. Less than a
week.

She'd been in his company a total of three times,
and she was thinking of having sex with him.

*Be honest. You're doing more than thinking. You're
planning to have sex with him tonight, and you know
it. You knew it the second you said you'd come here
tonight, and he knows it, too. Besides, why else did
you wear those blue lace undies—the ones you got from
Liz last Christmas and have never worn?*

"Shawn?"

Reluctantly she faced him.

His smile was tender. "Would you like a glass of
wine?"

She nodded. "That sounds good." She needed *something*, that was for sure. She was so wired, she felt as if she might explode. She couldn't remember ever being so nervous before. What if she was a dismal failure tonight? What if he could hardly wait for her to leave? What if she so disappointed him, he never wanted to see her again?

Michael walked off toward the kitchen, and Shawn laid her purse and sweater at one end of the sofa. Wiping her sweaty palms against the sides of her slacks, she took a couple more deep breaths.

She had to settle down. After all, what was the big deal about this, anyway? Thousands, probably millions, of people had sex every single day. If they were all this nervous, the entire universe would be shaking.

She almost laughed aloud at the absurd picture she'd conjured. She had a sudden mental image of millions of people all bobbing up and down because the earth under their feet was so unsteady from all those jangled nerves.

"Well, I'm glad to see you smiling," Michael said, walking back into the living area. He handed her a glass of white wine.

Shawn sipped. The wine tasted good, not too sweet but not so dry it wrinkled her nose.

Michael motioned toward the sofa, and she sat down. She expected him to sit in the navy chair across from her. Instead he sat down beside her, with only inches separating them. He looked terrific tonight, she thought, in baggy olive drab pants and a chest-hugging black T-shirt. Casual, yet sophisticated. Stylish, yet very manly.

"Do I pass inspection?" he said dryly.

Shawn blushed. "Was I that obvious?" she managed to say lightly.

He grinned. Then the smile faded, and he said softly, "You look awfully pretty tonight." His eyes were warm as they appraised her.

"Thanks." She raised her wineglass and took another sip. How did people *do* this sort of thing? Her stupid heart was going sixty miles an hour, her hands were sweaty, her stomach was heaving, and she didn't know where to look.

She was a complete mess. At that moment, she desperately wanted to go home. Go home and forget all about this. Who needed it?

Michael set his wineglass down. He reached for hers, taking it from her suddenly nerveless fingers. Then he slipped his arm around her shoulders and raised her chin so that she had to look at him. His eyes were a smoky golden-brown in the lowering afternoon sunlight.

What is he doing? Shawn's heart fluttered in her chest as he brushed his lips across hers in a featherlight touch.

She trembled and closed her eyes, sighing as his lips settled softly against hers. He kissed her again and pulled her closer to him, and she placed her hands on his chest, feeling the warmth and hard, male contours under her palms. She could also feel his heart beating, its rhythm echoing her own increasing tempo.

"Shawn, you're so sweet," he whispered. "So sweet." He kissed her again, then again—tantalizing kisses that promised more but were not demanding. Not yet.

With his free hand he caressed her hair and her cheek, continuing to feather kisses over her face. "Do you know what you do to me?" he whispered between kisses. "Do you have any idea?"

Shawn couldn't have answered if her life had depended upon it. But he didn't seem to require an answer as he feathered kisses over her eyes and cheeks.

His hand glided down to her neck and rested there for a moment, then moved unerringly to cover her right breast. Shawn shuddered as he molded it to the shape of his hand, then stroked her. At the same time he deepened his kiss, and his tongue, hard and strong, invaded her mouth, claiming her and demanding a response.

Her entire body arched as she blossomed under his kiss and his insistent touch, and something hot spiraled through her, centering deep in her body, throbbing and aching and crying out for fulfillment.

"I want you, Shawn," he whispered against her mouth. "Do you still want me?"

"Yes," she said on a sigh as his thumb circled her breast.

Without another word, he scooped her up into his arms and stood. Without giving her time to think or doubt, he kissed her hard, then looked deeply into her eyes for one long moment. When she made no objection, he held her close to his chest and walked toward the stairs.

Shawn clung to him as he carried her up the stairs and into his bedroom. She tried not to think. She knew if she thought too much, she'd get scared again. And she didn't want to be frightened. If she was going to do this, she wanted to know what she was doing. She wanted to enjoy it and remember it and do it wholeheartedly.

She wanted to be a woman.

She wanted to be responsible for her choices.

And she didn't want to disappoint Michael.

When they reached his bedroom, he set her down, but he still held her close.

He kissed her again. And again. Kisses designed to keep her head spinning and her desire raging.

Long minutes later he murmured, "Wait a minute. Don't move." He walked over to the only window in the room and closed the blinds, then drew the drapes.

Now the room was filled with a shadowy red-gold light that lent a dreamy quality to the scene.

He turned back to her, walking slowly. When he reached her, he smiled. Something inside Shawn twisted in response. Slowly, as if they were in a slow-motion film, he reached for the buttons on her blouse. Shawn couldn't move, couldn't breathe. She also couldn't look away. His eyes never left her face as he slowly undid the buttons, then opened her blouse.

"Shawn," he whispered. With his fingertips, he gently touched her chest, then the swell of her breasts over the tops of the lacy bra. Shawn's heart beat in slow thuds as he unhooked the front of the bra and slowly laid it back.

When he touched her, something inside Shawn skyrocketed and she trembled violently. Michael immediately pulled her into his arms and held her tight. He pushed her hair away from her neck, and dropped his warm, moist mouth to the hollow. Shawn's breasts tingled from the contact with his T-shirt, and heat spiraled through her as Michael's mouth trailed down further.

Suddenly he was no longer moving slow.

Or quite as gently.

With a guttural sound, he shoved her blouse off her shoulders, then pulled her bra away from her body. He walked her backwards toward the bed, then, using his body as a lever, laid her down and lay on top of her.

Shawn gasped as she felt the heat of him against her body. Instinctively she spread her legs open, and he settled against her—hard and hot and pulsing. Her body reacted immediately to this stimulus with an answering fire.

Michael palmed her bare breasts, kneading and teasing, as his mouth covered hers with open, demanding kisses. Within moments, Shawn was responding with the same demand. All shyness, all uncertainty, had vanished under the spell of Michael's hands and mouth.

The only thought in Shawn's head was that she wanted him. She wanted him inside her.

Now.

Before she knew how it had happened, Michael had unzipped her slacks, and she was helping him slide them down. Then she helped him take off his T-shirt and slip off the baggy pants. Shawn stared, awed by his body's response, knowing it was due to her and the way he was feeling about her.

He *did* want her!

A powerful feeling washed over her, and all the last remnants of her fear disappeared.

Michael lay down beside her, reaching for a pillow and placing it under her head. They were angled sideways across the bed, and for the first time Shawn realized the bedspread was folded at the bottom, and they were lying on the sheet. She knew she should be embarrassed or something at the thought that Michael had prepared for this. Instead, she was grateful to him for making everything so easy. And so natural.

She turned on her side to face him, and he began to touch her again. Boldly she imitated his moves. When he touched her breasts, making her gasp with a quick intake of breath, she did the same thing, feeling the springy hair of his chest and the strong beat of his heart under her palms. And when he moaned softly, she smiled.

When his hand drifted lower, stroking her belly, she explored his body, too. She loved the way he was making her feel, but she also loved touching him.

But when his fingers slid under the waistband of her panties, she suddenly forgot about everything but what Michael was doing to her. He touched her intimately, and over her hammering heartbeat, she could feel a strange coiling sensation deep inside her. She moaned. "Shhh," he said, exploring until he centered on that tiny place that seemed to be the exact spot where all the feeling in her body was located.

Shawn felt as if she were at the top of a very high cliff. Her body was wracked with sensations. "Wait, wait," she protested, knowing that any minute she was going to topple over the edge, and she wanted Michael with her when she did. She tried to twist away from him, tried to touch him, but he wouldn't let her.

"Not yet," he muttered thickly. "This first . . ." And he kept up the exquisite torture. Shawn could feel herself leaning toward the abyss. She gripped his shoulders tightly as she teetered on the edge, then, in a burst of pleasure, her body exploded and she began to fall, hurtling through space in a freefall of sensations so powerful, they took her breath away.

He held her until she calmed. "Now," he said against her ear, "you can touch me."

And she did, feeling the heat of him against her palm, marveling at the leashed power she felt.

"Let's get rid of these," he said, and slid her panties

down. Then he removed his briefs, and now he pulled her close, and she could feel all of him against her, and it was a wonderful feeling.

He began to stroke her back and kiss her again. Soon her body began to respond in the same way it had responded before. When the heat began to build again, he laid her back and very slowly, he entered her.

He felt wonderful inside her—hot and heavy and right—as if he belonged there. And as he moved and she matched her moves to his, she crept closer and closer to the edge of that cliff once more. Then, suddenly, she was there, and a second later, he was, too. As great shudders wracked his body, Shawn clung to him, closing her eyes and letting herself fall with him.

She had no more doubts. No more fears. Here, at this moment, with this man, she felt completely safe. *I love him*, she thought. *I love him, and even if he doesn't love me, it's okay. Even if I never have more than this, I'll never be sorry.*

A long time later, as Shawn lay wrapped in Michael's arms, her head tucked under his chin, he whispered, "You're wonderful, do you know that?"

"I am?" she said, happiness sailing through her.

"Yes." He kissed her forehead, then her nose, his warm breath drifting across her face. "Innocent yet sexy. Shy yet bold. Ladylike yet seductive."

"All that?" she teased.

"All that. And more." His hand rested on her breast. "And what about me? Has your opinion of me changed?"

"You mean, since tonight?"

He chuckled, the sound causing pleasure to ripple through her. "Yes, I mean, since tonight."

"Well . . ."

He tweaked her nose. "Come on, woman. I asked you a question. Don't play games."

"But games are fun, don't you think?"

He laughed, then gave her a lingering kiss. "Some games are more fun than others," he murmured. "Now answer my question."

She relented. "I don't know if I'd say my opinion of you has changed, exactly. I mean, I always thought you were sexy."

"You did?"

She smiled. She heard the pleased expression in his voice. "Uh-huh. And I always thought you were handsome."

She could feel his smile against her forehead as he settled his arms more comfortably around her. "And I knew you were nice," she continued softly.

"Nice. Hmmm. Nice."

"And now . . ."

"Yes?"

She smiled. "Now I think you're an absolutely fabulous lover."

She could almost feel his chest swelling, and her smile expanded to a grin.

"You do?" he finally said.

"Yes, I do."

He pulled her tightly against him, and his mouth found her ear. He kissed her there, then whispered huskily, "Well, if I'm such a fabulous lover, it's because I've got such a wonderful partner." He laughed softly. "They say practice makes perfect, you know."

"Do they?" She trembled as he continued to kiss her ear and neck.

"Yep, that's what they say. So we should probably try to get more practice in, don't you think?"

"Tonight?" she said breathlessly.

"How does tonight and tomorrow night and every night from now on sound?" he whispered.

"Every night?"

"Well, maybe on Sunday nights I'll let you rest."

"That's big of you."

He chuckled. "Something else is big of me, too."

"Michael!"

"However," he said, still laughing softly, "I'm going to try to contain myself, at least for the next hour or so, because I'm starving. So why don't we get up and order that pizza?" He touched the lobe of her ear with his tongue. "And all the while we're eating, we can think about making love." His voice was low and husky and filled with promise. "We can look at each other and know we're going to make love again, and that'll make it all the better when we finally do."

"It will?" she whispered.

"Oh, yes. Trust me. It will."

He would never get tired of looking at her, Michael decided as he watched Shawn lift a stray sliver of mozzarella cheese and place it carefully on top of her pizza slice. She took a bite of the pizza and chewed slowly.

It was nine o'clock, and they were sitting on the floor in the living room. Shawn was wrapped in his navy blue terry cloth robe. Her red-gold hair, disheveled and tumbling over her shoulders, gleamed in the lamplight. Most of her makeup was gone, and her mouth looked swollen and delectable from their lovemaking.

Each time they looked at each other, he saw the awareness in her eyes. The awareness and the anticipation, and he knew she was remembering what he'd said.

Thinking about making love with him again. He wondered if she was already hot and slick and ready for him. His breathing accelerated as he thought about all the ways he wanted to love her.

He smiled at her, letting his gaze travel slowly over her body, remembering its feel under his hands and mouth, remembering its response to his touches and kisses. He could feel the anticipation building, and he could hardly wait to get his hands on her again. Yet he knew the waiting would make the next time so much better.

Her robe had fallen open a bit, and he could just see the swell of her breast half-hidden in its folds. God, she was beautiful, he thought. He liked everything about her, from the top of her curly head to the bottoms of her slender feet with their pretty little toes. As he watched, she wriggled them, and he decided he'd love to see if they tasted as good as they looked.

"Why are you staring at my feet?" she asked.

Michael grinned. "I was thinking how delicious your toes look." Then he laughed out loud when he saw her face flame. He loved it that she blushed so easily. It was very refreshing to be around a woman who actually got embarrassed when he flirted with her or said something mildly suggestive.

She hurriedly ate some more of her pizza. "Let's drop the subject of my toes, okay?"

"Why? Does it make you uncomfortable that I think every inch of you is beautiful?" Michael set his pizza slice down.

"I . . . not exactly . . ." She squirmed and tried to cover her feet with the edge of the robe, but it wouldn't quite reach.

"What is it then? Why are you so embarrassed?"

"It's nothing!" There was a note of panic in her voice.

"I don't think it's nothing, Shawn. And you might as well tell me, because I'm not going to drop the subject." He inched over until he was sitting in front of her. He touched her left foot, lifting it in his hand.

He rubbed it slowly, letting his thumb massage the undersole. Then he slowly kissed it, never taking his eyes from hers.

Shawn's throat worked, and she laid her slice of pizza down. "Michael," she said weakly. "What are you doing?" But there was no note of protest in her voice.

"I'm going to make love to you, starting with these pretty little toes," he said.

"You are?" Her eyes drifted shut as he began to do just that. Yes, they *did* taste as good as they looked, he thought, watching Shawn's face. "Did you like that?" he whispered when he was finished and began to slowly slide his hands up her legs.

Her voice sounded breathless as she said, "I . . . I loved it. It . . . it was the fulfillment of one my fantasies."

And just before he opened her robe, he said, "Tell me what your other fantasies are. Maybe we can fulfill all of them."

Much later, after Shawn had admitted to him that Annika wasn't at home, Michael gathered up his uniform and, when Shawn didn't object, told her he'd go home with her and they could get ready for work together.

Shawn's eyes widened when he suggested they shower together.

"Humor me, okay?" He grinned. "That's one of *my* fantasies."

"Again?" she said later as, bodies covered with lather from soaping each other, he lifted her up and settled her atop him.

"Now, isn't that nice?" he said as the hot water beat down on them and he was enfolded inside her.

"Very nice," she agreed.

Still later, as he watched her comb her hair, she suddenly stopped, and their eyes met in the mirror. Something about her expression disturbed him, and for a moment he felt afraid. Was she sorry? Did she somehow suspect that he was hiding something from her?

But then his fear faded, for she smiled and said softly, "No matter what happens in the future, Michael, I just wanted you to know that I have no regrets about tonight."

And in that moment, Michael knew that somehow, some way, he had to figure out how to keep Shawn feeling that way, especially when she found out who he really was.

NINE

Shawn didn't want to walk into the casino with Michael. "I'm sorry," she explained as they pulled into the employees' parking lot. "I just feel a little funny about it." She gave him an apologetic smile. "It has nothing to do with you."

"It's okay," Michael said. "I'll just wait outside for a few minutes. You go on in."

She stood on tiptoe and kissed him, and Michael held her close for a second. He watched her walk away, thinking even in her uniform consisting of trim black skirt, white satin blouse, and black velvet bolero, she looked good to him.

After she'd disappeared inside, he gave her five minutes to punch in, then strolled toward the employee entrance. He signed in with the security guard, then headed for the rack of time cards.

He reached for his, then frowned. There was a note clipped to the back. He unfolded it. It read: "I'll be in my office when you arrive at midnight. Come see me on your first break, and be careful." It was signed with just an initial: D.

Dominic. His godfather.

Michael's frown deepened. What did Dominic want to see him about? What was so important it couldn't wait until tomorrow morning? Had something happened?

Worried, he ran his hands through his hair. Something must have gone wrong. Damn! Didn't he have *enough* to worry about with Shawn?

Shawn.

Thank God she had insisted on walking in alone. What if she'd been here? Seen the note? What would he have said if she'd asked about it?

Michael silently berated his godfather. Dominic had certainly taken a foolish chance. And why? What was so all-fired important that his godfather couldn't have waited to call Michael at home?

Mind whirling with unanswered questions, he punched in, then headed for the locker room. After stowing his things, he walked out onto the casino floor. When he entered the blackjack pit, he discovered he'd been assigned to the other end of the pit from where Shawn was working. He decided that was probably for the best. He wasn't sure how well he'd concentrate if he was too close to her tonight. It was bad enough that he had that damned summons to think about.

"Hey, how's it going?" said Floyd Hazlett, who was his partner for the shift. His big face creased into a smile.

Michael smiled back. He liked Floyd and hoped he wasn't involved in the skimming operation. A country boy, Floyd had grown up on a ranch in northern Nevada. He'd told Michael that his father still worked the ranch, but it barely broke even. Floyd was big and rawboned and on the quiet side.

"Great," Michael said. "How's it going with you, Floyd?"

"I'm not complaining. Hey, are we still on for golf this weekend?"

"You bet."

The shift wasn't as busy as swing shift had been the previous week, but still Michael found little time for thinking about Shawn or worrying about his godfather's summons. When his first break came, he was grateful to see that Shawn wasn't on the same break schedule tonight. That was lucky. He didn't want to hurt her feelings *or* make her curious about why he wasn't spending his break with her.

Michael took off for the stairs at a fast clip. He only had fifteen minutes.

No one noticed him going upstairs, he was sure of that. When he arrived at Dominic's office on the fourth floor, the halls were deserted. So far, so good.

Reaching Dominic's office, he rapped softly.

"Come on in," Dominic called.

"What was so important you took a chance writing me a note here?" he said, dropping into one of the leather chairs flanking Dominic's big desk.

"I had to. Something very strange happened today," Dominic said, worry lines creasing his forehead. "And I wanted you to know about it right away, just in case . . ."

"Just in case, what?"

"Well, this afternoon, right before Evelyn was ready to go home, Philip Brownlee stopped by." Evelyn was Dominic's secretary.

"So?"

Dominic steepled his hands, his frown deepening. "He wanted your personnel file."

"My personnel file?" Now Michael frowned, too. "Why would he want to see my personnel file?"

"I don't know. The thing is, you don't have a file, so we've got to come up with one. And quick."

"I wonder if this has anything to do with Shawn," Michael said thoughtfully.

"I have no idea, but it doesn't matter, does it? He told Evelyn he'd been to Personnel and asked to see the files on all the new hires, and they'd given him all but yours. Unfortunately, instead of telling him they couldn't locate your file right then, that fool in Personnel told him I must have it."

"So what did Evelyn say?"

"She told Brownlee she'd ask me about it. Luckily, when he came, I was on a conference call, so she told him she'd get back to him tomorrow."

Michael thought for a moment. "Do you think Brownlee is suspicious?"

"Your guess is as good as mine," Dominic said. "But the fact remains, he's asked to see your file."

"Tell you what. Have Evelyn stall Brownlee if he comes up again tomorrow. Just tell her you thought you'd returned my file to Personnel. Act like you've misplaced it, and tell her you'll look for it later. Tell her to tell Brownlee it might be a day or two before she'll have it. And in the meantime, call Dad and ask him to have his people prepare a phony file for me."

"Okay." Dominic studied him. "How did things go with the MacInnes woman last night?"

"Fine."

"Did you learn anything else?"

"No," Michael said curtly. "And I don't expect to. I told you. I'm sure she has nothing to do with this."

"For your sake, I hope you're right," Dominic said softly.

Michael stiffened. "Why do you say that?"

"Because the way you act every time the woman's name is mentioned, it's obvious to me that you've taken a personal interest in her."

Michael couldn't deny what he knew was true.

"Be careful, Michael," Dominic warned.

"I'm always careful."

"Sometimes even careful men can do foolish things when it comes to a woman."

"Don't worry about me." Michael stood. "Listen, I don't have time to talk about this any longer. My break'll be up in exactly three minutes. I'd better go."

But as he hurried back to the floor, he couldn't get his godfather's warning out of his mind.

When the shift was over, Shawn waited for Michael, and they walked out together. "I thought you didn't want to be seen with me," he teased.

She shrugged. "I decided I was being silly. Why *shouldn't* I be seen with you?"

He smiled and slipped his arm around her shoulders. After signing out, they exited the back door, and Shawn blinked against the bright early morning sun.

If she lived to be one hundred, she'd never get used to the contrast between the dark casino and the natural outdoor light. She knew the casinos were deliberately kept dark so the customers would lose track of time.

That was the reason Las Vegas was the city without clocks. The city fathers wanted the tourists to gamble twenty-four hours a day. The more money they left in the casinos, the more tax revenues that would find their way into the coffers of the state of Nevada as well as the city.

They walked slowly to Michael's car. He unlocked the passenger door and helped her in. Then he climbed in on his side. As he turned the ignition, he glanced over at her, and in a husky voice said, "My place or yours?"

Shawn's pulse quickened and her gaze met his. "Michael, I have so many things to do—"

"Do them later. Let's go to my place and go to bed." He skillfully maneuvered the Corvette out of its parking slot. He squeezed her knee gently. "I'll even let you sleep . . . after a while. . . ."

They went to his place.

During the next two and a half weeks, Shawn spent more time at Michael's place then she did at her own. It was one of the happiest periods of her life, filled with experiences she knew she'd remember forever.

Michael.

He was wonderful.

She couldn't believe how much fun they had together. From the time she was a little girl, she'd always been too serious, and she knew it. She hadn't wanted to be that way, but she hadn't known how to be any different.

Shawn was shy, and shy people didn't know how to relax and enjoy themselves around other people because they were too self-conscious and too afraid.

With Michael, Shawn felt like a different person. She felt prettier and more vivacious. She felt witty and clever and lighthearted.

And she felt sexy.

Oh, boy, did she feel sexy.

She reveled in her newfound sensuality. She could almost feel herself emerging, like a butterfly, from the cocoon that had inhibited and confined her all her life.

It was so wonderful to have someone like Michael to share things with. Now when she read something funny—like her favorite Calvin and Hobbes cartoons— she could read them aloud to Michael, and they could laugh together.

When she saw something on TV or heard something on the radio that she found particularly interesting, she could discuss it with Michael. He didn't always agree with her views, and even that was all right. Arguing a point was fun when you were arguing with someone you respected and loved.

She loved him.

Shawn hugged the knowledge to herself.

She loved him so much, it scared her.

When she was with him, she felt wrapped in happiness.

When she was with him, she didn't feel lonely. She didn't feel like an outsider.

She belonged.

She belonged with Michael.

When he touched her, it was like setting a match to dry wood. She immediately blazed into flames, and Michael knew just how to stoke that fire until it became a raging inferno of sensation.

When they were together, she felt invincible. As if nothing could touch her. As if nothing could harm her. As if nothing bad would ever happen to her again.

The intensity of her feelings for Michael permeated every area of her life. Made every experience richer and better.

Her painting improved. She'd always been good. She knew that. But now her paintings were inspired. They were filled with color and light and joy.

The sun seemed to shine brighter. The birdsong seemed more beautiful. All the colors in the universe shone with more luster and clarity.

She drifted through the days and nights in a haze of happiness and heightened awareness of the world around her.

The only dark spot on her horizon was the fact that Michael never mentioned the future. When she let herself think about the future, she got scared, because what if, after showing her how impossibly wonderful life could be with him, he simply disappeared one day?

What if, when it came time for her to leave Las Vegas, he let her go without a word to stop her?

When these questions hammered at her, some of her joy was diminished, so she tried not to think about them. She tried to empty her mind of everything but the present. She told herself she would live her life to the fullest and not worry about what might or might not happen tomorrow.

Shawn had always planned everything down to the last detail, made lists as automatically as some people draw breath. But now she stopped planning, and she stopped worrying.

She savored each moment.

With Michael, she did all the things she'd never taken the time to do before.

One morning they packed a picnic lunch and spent the day at Lake Mead. They napped on a blanket in the sun, Michael's arm lying across Shawn's waist. Every once in awhile he would lift his head and kiss her, and she'd look into his topaz eyes and think how lucky she was. They'd smile at each other, then they'd both doze again.

At noon they roused themselves to eat lunch—cold fried chicken; firm, sweet red grapes; and hunks of French bread slathered with butter. Then, replete from the sunshine and food, they drove back to Michael's place, where they spent a long, lazy afternoon in bed— first making love, then sleeping, then making love again.

Another day, when Annika stayed over at Darryl's, Shawn and Michael spent the morning at her place, where he lounged in a beanbag chair and watched her paint. "You're really good, you know that?" he said, and she smiled. Their gazes met and held, and Shawn's breath caught suddenly. Within minutes, they were making love.

They always seemed to be making love. They couldn't seem to get enough of each other.

Sometimes Shawn had to pinch herself as a reminder that what was happening was real, not something she'd dreamed up to fill the empty spot in her life.

Michael was the perfect lover, the perfect friend. He had that rare ability to make even the simplest experience special.

He took her to the movies and they held hands and gorged themselves on buttered popcorn and chocolate malt balls.

He took her bowling and they both laughed when she threw a gutter ball.

And one afternoon, over her halfhearted protests, he took her to a lingerie shop, where he picked out the most seductive and naughty-looking undergarments Shawn had ever seen.

"I can hardly wait to see you in this," he whispered

in her ear as he held up a black lace garter belt with tiny pink satin rosettes on the end of each garter.

Shawn blushed.

But that night, she wore the garter belt.

The sex was wonderful. Fantastic, even. But it wasn't just the sex that caused Shawn to fall into daydreams at odd moments throughout the days or catch herself humming while she worked.

Every day, in every way, Michael showed her he cared about her.

Yet he never told her he loved her.

And because he hadn't said the words, Shawn couldn't say them, either.

She told herself it didn't matter that he couldn't admit to his feelings for her.

She told herself that even if he never said he loved her, having this time with him was enough.

She told herself that even if he left her, or called their relationship off, she could handle it.

But she knew she was lying. She knew she would be devastated if Michael, for whatever reason, disappeared from her life. He had become a part of her, and if he were to go away, she would no longer be a whole person.

She no longer cared who knew how she felt about him. When Annika or Liz teased her, she just smiled. When her mother called one day and the conversation turned to Michael, Shawn freely and happily told her mother they were seeing a lot of each other.

All her doubts about him had vanished. It was almost anticlimactic when her uncle called her one day to say Michael had checked out perfectly. "There doesn't seem to be any reason to worry," he assured her. "I had a chance to talk to him personally the other day, too.''

"Yes, I know. He told me.''

"He impressed me. He seems intelligent and direct. Jimmy Penner also tells me he's a good worker.''

Shawn glowed as if her uncle were praising her instead of Michael.

Before they hung up, her uncle said he'd like to take her and Michael out to dinner one night. "Your mother and I would enjoy that very much.''

"It'll have to wait awhile,'' Shawn said. "We both start the afternoon shift tomorrow.''

"Why don't we make a date for your next day off?''

Shawn wasn't sure she was ready for this. "I'll have to ask Michael,'' she hedged.

"You do that. And in the meantime, I'll talk to your mother. I'm looking forward to this, Shawn.''

Michael knew he was flirting with disaster. He knew it, but he couldn't seem to help himself. He tried to keep his mind on the job at hand, but more and more, the only important thing in his life was Shawn. Nothing else seemed to matter, and he refused to think about what would happen when Shawn found out who he was and why he was really in Las Vegas.

Somehow, in some way, things would work out.

They *had* to work out.

He only wished he were making some progress in his investigation. So far, he'd discovered nothing useful. About the only thing conclusive he'd come up with was that whether it was Philip Brownlee or someone else masterminding this operation, he had to have help. Because of the elaborate safeguards and security measures taken in all phases of the casino, it would be virtually impossible for one employee to steal.

The only way a single employee could steal—at least as far as Michael could see—was if a crooked dealer, working in conjunction with a friend, overpaid that friend in winnings.

But Michael couldn't see how any one dealer could do that kind of thing very often. First of all, it would cause suspicion for the same person to play at the same dealer's table day after day, and secondly, a dealer couldn't pay off too much more than a player was supposed to get without someone noticing. There were hundreds of mirrors in the ceiling of the casino, and the dealers and croupiers were constantly watched.

No, Michael thought, that kind of thing would be penny-ante. There also was no way to steal when money was brought to the tables from the cashier's office, because the transfer of money required three signatures at The Glass Slipper. The first sign-off occurred at the cashier's office, where the cashier, the security guard, and the floorman all watched the money being counted and signed off on the total. Then when the money was taken to the dealer's table, the dealer, the floorman, and the pit boss all signed off on the amount.

As far as Michael could see, the only time any significant amount of money could be taken was when the cash was removed from the lock boxes under the dealers' tables and taken to the cashier's office for counting. As he'd told his godfather, this was the most vulnerable time for the casino.

The actual counting involved three people. The pit boss, the security guard, and the head cashier on duty that shift.

If whoever had been stealing in the past continued

to steal, and if that stealing took place during the counting of the proceeds from the gaming tables, they would soon know. The camera Michael had suggested they install had been put in place the previous day. Michael didn't think anyone would be suspicious about it, either, because as he'd suggested, the installation was done under cover of painting the room.

Michael had also decided to try to determine whether there was any pattern in the size of previous pickups. Whether, when any three people were involved, the revenues seemed to be less. So for the past week, Michael had had one of his father's analysts studying the records of all the hourly pickups for the past year. It would be another week before the data was summarized and available.

Except for spending time with Shawn's uncle, Philip Brownlee, Michael had done everything he could think of to do. And even that would soon be remedied. He and Shawn had been invited to have dinner with her mother and her uncle as soon as their current shift was over. And that would be in three days, when they'd have Saturday through Monday off.

Saturday night he would have a chance to study Philip Brownlee in a relaxed atmosphere. He could ask some careful questions and assess the man at close range.

He refused to think about what would happen if it turned out that Philip Brownlee was involved in this mess.

On Saturday night Shawn put the finishing touches to her makeup and inspected herself in the mirror.

Was this wise? she asked herself. Wouldn't taking Michael to meet her family make everything all the harder if, for some reason, she and Michael broke up? It would be especially difficult if Michael were the one to terminate their relationship.

Shawn knew that a breakup would be hard enough to survive, but having other people know about it—especially her mother and uncle—would make it almost unbearable. Bad enough to be heartbroken, but to have to endure the pitying looks of people you loved would be sheer torture.

She sighed, smoothing down the skirt of her navy blue dress. Well, it was too late now. The die was cast. She and Michael were having dinner with her mother and her uncle tonight. In fact, Michael would pick her up in less than twenty minutes.

Carolyn had insisted on cooking dinner for all of them, so when Michael came, looking terrific to Shawn in his open-necked tan shirt and matching slacks worn with a dark blue blazer, they headed for her mother's house.

When they arrived, Carolyn greeted them at the door. She smiled. "So you're Michael," she said. "I've heard a lot about you."

"And I've heard a lot about you."

Just then Philip walked up behind Carolyn, and she turned. "Philip, you've met Michael, haven't you?"

"Yes, we've met. Hi, Michael." He extended his hand, and Michael took it.

A few minutes later, Michael and Philip, drinks in hand, were settled in the living room, and Shawn followed her mother to the kitchen.

"What can I do to help?" Shawn asked.

"Well, you can slice that loaf of French bread while I check the casserole." Her mother opened the oven and peered inside.

Shawn did as she was told while studying her mother. Carolyn looked great, Shawn thought, in a flowing, wide-legged pants outfit made out of some kind of silky material in a beautiful shade of raspberry. It was a color Shawn could never have worn, not with her hair.

She sighed, hoping when she was her mother's age, she'd look half as good.

When all the food was ready and on the dining room table, they summoned the men.

Shawn was feeling a little more relaxed by now and had almost decided her earlier uneasiness had been silly. She relaxed even more as the dinner progressed, but not completely. She was too aware of Michael seated across from her. Her feelings for him were too new and too exciting. She wanted her mother and her uncle to like him, too.

"So, Michael, Shawn tells me you're from New York?" her mother said.

Michael's gaze met Shawn's for a moment, then he turned to her mother. "Yes. I grew up on Long Island."

"I've only visited New York once," Carolyn said. "And that was when Gerald and I were first married. I loved it."

"Yes, it's a great place to visit," Michael said.

"I know Shawn's really looking forward to going," Carolyn said. "Aren't you, honey?"

Michael looked at Shawn in surprise. "I didn't know you were planning to go to New York."

She shrugged. "Well, it's not definite or anything, but, you know, I'm planning to move east . . . and I thought I'd spend a couple of days in the city on the way to New England. I mean, it would be a shame to be so close and not visit the museums and galleries.''

Michael nodded thoughtfully, his eyes enigmatic, and she wondered what he was thinking. Funny, the thought of visiting New York had been so exciting to her just scant weeks ago. Now, since meeting Michael, all that had changed. Even the prospect of visiting the Metropolitan and the other museums she'd only dreamed of seeing failed to elicit any enthusiasm.

How could she be enthusiastic about the prospect of leaving Michael? she thought bleakly. The realization was sobering. Even her goal of moving east, taking a year to paint, didn't hold the same kind of appeal for her it once had.

"I understand your father is a friend of Mr. Cassione,'' Philip said.

Shawn's gaze darted to Michael. Was he? Michael had never mentioned that.

"Who told you that?'' Michael asked.

Her uncle frowned. "I can't remember now, but I was sure someone said so.''

"It's true that my father has connections here,'' Michael said, "and he used them to help me find a job.''

"Remember, Michael, it's juice, not connections,'' Shawn said lightly, but she wondered if her uncle had noticed that Michael hadn't really answered his question.

Michael grinned. "I forgot. Juice.''

Carolyn laughed. "I see Shawn is educating you as far as Las Vegas terminology is concerned.''

"So what does your father do?'' Philip asked.

Shawn shifted uncomfortably. Was her uncle pumping Michael, or was that her imagination?

The question didn't seem to bother Michael. "He's

involved in commercial real estate and putting together big financial deals," he said easily.

Her uncle nodded. "You didn't want to work for him, I take it?"

"I'm tired of working for him," Michael said. "It's time for me to do something on my own." He looked at Shawn. "Like Shawn, I have a dream."

Shawn met his gaze. *Oh, Michael, if you only knew it, but my dream has changed since meeting you.* She wondered if he had any idea how his introduction into her life had altered it. Had altered *her*.

Suddenly pensive, she looked away. She busied herself eating the rest of her dinner, but the insidious thought refused to disappear.

She had changed irrevocably since meeting Michael.

Nothing would ever be the same again.

After dinner, Shawn stood at the sink and rinsed dirty dishes while Carolyn loaded the dishwasher.

"Shawn, I *really* like Michael," Carolyn said, looking up with a smile.

"Do you?" Shawn handed her another dish.

"Yes. Very much. And I think Philip does, too."

Shawn nodded thoughtfully.

Carolyn's hands stilled. "Is something wrong?"

Shawn shrugged. "I hope not."

"Shawn, what is it?" her mother said softly.

"I wish I knew how Michael feels about me."

"Is that all?" Carolyn chuckled. "It's obvious. He's crazy about you!"

Shawn wished she could believe that. Sometimes she did, but tonight, after the talk about New York and her going to New England, she was riddled with doubts. If only Michael would *say* he was crazy about her. If only he would say something, anything, about the future. She bit her lip to still the sudden trembling.

"Honey . . ." Her mother touched her arm. "Surely you're not *worried* about how he feels. Are you?"

Shawn's chest felt tight. Meeting her mother's gaze, she whispered, "I love him, Mom. And I'm afraid he doesn't love me."

Carolyn put down the dish she was holding and pulled Shawn close. "He loves you," she murmured. "All you have to do is see the way he looks at you to know he loves you."

"I wish I could believe that."

"Believe it."

"Then why hasn't he *said* so?"

Carolyn gently touched Shawn's hair back and looked into her eyes. "Darling, give him time. Most men don't give up their freedom lightly. Just be patient."

Be patient.

Later that night, as Shawn lay in bed next to a sleeping Michael, she thought about her mother's advice. She knew it was sound advice. She knew her relationship with Michael was still too new for either of them to be sure about where it was going. She knew it was better for both of them to take their time before moving on to the next phase of their relationship.

Right now she supposed she should be content with the status quo. But things couldn't remain this way indefinitely.

Sooner or later, some kind of decision had to be made.

Either they would go forward and deepen their relationship.

Or Michael would leave her.

Her last thought before falling asleep was that whatever happened, she hoped she would be able to deal with it.

TEN

Shawn was tired. She glanced at her watch. Still two more hours to go before her shift was over.

She sighed. Coming back to work after three days off was always hard.

She rubbed the back of her neck as she waited for one of the players at her table to make up her mind if she wanted another card. Her exposed card was the king of spades. She kept looking at Shawn's exposed card, the eight of spades.

Finally she flipped her other card over.

It was the king of hearts.

The woman grinned. "I want to split my bet," she said triumphantly.

Shawn groaned inwardly. Only a novice player would do what the woman had done. Two face cards were an almost sure winner. Now the woman had doubled her chances of losing. But there was nothing Shawn could do except honor the woman's wishes.

Shawn dealt her a card to go with the first king. The

three of clubs. The woman frowned and indicated she wanted another. Shawn dealt her the nine of hearts.

The woman looked pained as Shawn moved to the king of hearts, and when she was dealt the seven of diamonds, instead of standing with that card and taking her chances, she panicked and motioned for another card. Inwardly shaking her head, Shawn dealt her the next card, the ten of spades.

Shawn sighed at the expression on the woman's face, especially when Shawn ended up going over twenty-one herself. Softly, as she gathered up the house winnings, she said, "Anytime you're dealt anything higher than two eights, don't split them."

From just over her shoulder, Michael's voice murmured into her ear, "Save us from small children and fools."

Shawn glanced back, and Michael winked at her, his golden-brown eyes filled with teasing glints. As the play of the next hand began, she could feel him there, only inches away, and the knowledge warmed her.

A few minutes later, the woman who had been playing so poorly got up and left Shawn's table. Several people were walking by, and one of them, a gorgeous blonde in a strapless green sequined evening dress, sank gracefully into the vacated seat. She smiled at Shawn, who smiled back. Then the blonde frowned, looking at something behind Shawn.

She continued to frown and craned her neck to see better.

"Is something wrong?" Shawn asked.

The blonde blinked. "Oh, no. I just saw someone I know, and it surprised me, that's all." She pointed, then smiled happily. "Yes! It *is* Michael. I can't believe it! This is the last place I'd have ever expected to see Michael Vellini. Does he work here?''

''Michael Vellini?'' Who was the blonde talking about? Shawn turned around. The blonde was pointing at Michael's retreating back. Shawn frowned. ''You must be mistaken. That's Michael DeNiro, and yes, he works here.'' She began to deal the next hand.

The blonde gave her a skeptical look, her blue eyes glittering with interest. ''Michael *DeNiro*? I don't think so. Not unless there are two Michaels in this world who look exactly alike.''

Shawn finished dealing the first card facedown, then began dealing the second card. She tried to shove down her foreboding, even though she *knew* the blonde was mistaken.

''Would you mind telling him that an old, *close* friend would like to say hi?'' the blonde said.

Shawn's stomach suddenly felt hollow. All her doubts about Michael—doubts she'd managed to bury—surfaced again. She nodded. ''When the hand's over, I will.''

They finished playing the hand, and Shawn paid off the winners. Then she turned. Michael was nowhere to be seen, but Jimmy Penner stood nearby.

''Jimmy,'' Shawn said, beckoning to him.

He walked over quickly.

''Uh . . . could you call Michael over?'' Shawn said. She inclined her head toward the blonde. ''She'd like to speak with him.''

''Okay. I'll get him.'' Jimmy walked off, and Shawn turned back to the table.

All the while Shawn dealt the next hand, her mind

churned. She kept looking at the beautiful blonde, comparing her spectacular good looks to her own quite ordinary looks. Who *was* this woman? What was going on? Why had she called Michael by another name? Shawn could hardly concentrate on the hand as she waited for Michael to come back to the table.

As soon as the hand was over, she looked around. She saw Michael and Jimmy a few feet away. Michael was shaking his head and looking in the direction of her table. Jimmy looked as if he was laughing. Shawn, with a sinking feeling, realized Michael didn't want to come over. And there could only be one reason for his reluctance. The blonde was right.

The blonde suddenly stood and waved. "Michael!" she called. "It's Cookie!"

Shawn told herself not to jump to conclusions, but it was hard not to when Michael finally walked over to the table, and Cookie whoever-she-was exclaimed happily, "Michael, it really *is* you! I couldn't believe it, but here you are, in the flesh, looking as handsome as ever!"

Michael avoided Shawn's eyes. "Hello, Cookie," he said quietly.

"What kind of welcome is that?" She threw her arms around him and kissed him full on the mouth. Then, laughing up at him, she said, "It's so good to *see* you. How long has it been? And what in the world are you doing here? I—"

Abruptly taking her arm, Michael said, "Listen, we're interrupting the play at the table. It's time for my break, so why don't we go have a drink at the bar and get caught up on old times?" Still avoiding Shawn's eyes, he hurried Cookie away.

Shawn stared after them. It was all she could do to pull her attention back to the table to resume dealing.

Her gaze kept drifting in the direction of the bar, where she could just glimpse the sheen of the sequins on Cookie's dress.

Shawn tried not to be upset. Tried not to jump to conclusions. Tried not to doubt Michael until he'd at least had a chance to explain.

But it was hard, because Michael had rushed Cookie away as if he didn't want anyone to hear anything else of what she had to say. Shawn had to ask herself why. If Michael had nothing to hide, he'd have had no reason to hurry Cookie off. He'd have stood there by the table and talked to her.

He didn't want me to hear.

As the minutes crawled by and Michael still didn't return to the pit, a cold fear crept through Shawn.

Why didn't he want me to hear what they said?

She wondered how he would behave when he returned to the pit. She knew she still wouldn't have any answers. She would have to wait until four o'clock, another two hours, when their shift would be over, before they'd have the privacy to talk.

He still hadn't returned when Shawn's relief came. Picking up her tokes, Shawn headed toward the lounge. She glanced at the bar as she walked by. Michael and the beautiful Cookie were sitting with their heads together.

Shawn hurried past. She escaped to the employee lounge, where she sat by herself and brooded. The more she thought about what had happened, the angrier she got. She no longer attempted to give Michael the benefit of the doubt. He was definitely hiding something. There was no other excuse for his actions.

He had a lot of explaining to do.

*   *   *

"You sure have a lot of explaining to do," Cookie said archly. "Why don't you want anyone to know you're Michael Vellini?"

"I told you," Michael said. "I'm doing some undercover work for my father. It would screw up everything if my cover is blown." When she looked as if she was going to continue protesting, he decided a little arm twisting might be in order. "You know my father, don't you, Cookie?" His voice was as smooth as butter. "The same father who owns a controlling interest in the studio you work for? I don't imagine you'd like to make him unhappy. . . ."

"Jeez, Michael! You don't have to be mean! Anyway, it's too late."

Michael stiffened. "What do you mean, it's too late?"

Cookie shrugged. "I'm sorry, but I *already* said you were Michael Vellini."

"To whom?"

"To that redheaded dealer."

Michael closed his eyes. Oh, great.

"I'm sorry, but how was I supposed to know?"

Shaking his head, Michael said, "You weren't."

"You're not gonna say anything to your father, are you?"

Michael sighed. "No. It's not your fault."

Cookie smiled happily. "Well, jeez, that's good. Now, come on. Tell me everything. I'm dying to know what's going on!"

"Look, Cookie, I can't talk any longer. I've got to get back to work."

"Well, what time do you get off work?"

"At four, but I've got an appointment then."

She laid her hand on his arm. "That's okay. Tonight would be better, anyway."

He gently removed her hand, then stood. He laid some money on the bar to pay for their drinks. "Sorry. I can't make it tonight, either."

"But, Michael! I'm only going to be in town one night! I want to spend some time with you."

"I can't, Cookie. Let's just leave it at that, okay?"

She frowned and looked as if she was going to say something else. Then she sighed. "Okay, Michael. It was nice seeing you again. Good luck."

When Michael got back to the pit, he didn't see Shawn anywhere. Relieved, he realized she'd gone on her break, so he had a few minutes to collect his thoughts before he had to face her.

What was he going to say to Shawn? How could he explain going by a name other than his own?

Michael stationed himself at the opposite end of the pit. He still hadn't decided what his story would be when he saw Shawn return from her break. He saw her search the pit, and he knew the moment she spied him. He couldn't avoid her any longer, so he walked over to her. "We need to talk," he said. "I'll meet you at the end of the shift, okay?"

She nodded, but there was no warmth in her eyes, and Michael felt a sinking sensation in his stomach.

For the rest of their shift he stayed as far away from her as he could. He didn't want to risk seeing that expression in her eyes again.

When the shift was over, he waited for her. She looked at him, but they didn't speak as they wove their way through the casino. When she headed for the locker room, he said, "I'll wait for you outside."

"Okay."

Michael waved to the guard on duty as he left the casino. It was a brilliantly beautiful day somewhere in the low sixties—perfect weather, Michael thought. He drew in deep breaths of the fresh air.

A few minutes later Shawn walked outside. The sun glinted off her glasses, which she always wore while working. Somehow, when she wore them, she always seemed more vulnerable to him. As she drew abreast of him, he said, "Do you want to come to my place to talk?"

"No, Michael. I want to talk right here."

"Here?"

"Yes. Here."

There was that cold expression again. Michael couldn't remember another time when Shawn had looked at him like that. And he certainly hoped she never looked like that again.

"We'd be a lot more comfortable at my place."

Her jaw jutted stubbornly. "I don't think so."

"Let's at least go sit in my car."

She gave him no further argument, but when he reached for her arm, she shrugged it off.

She also opened the car door herself.

I'm in really big trouble, Michael thought.

Once they were settled inside, Shawn turned to him. Her eyes behind her lenses looked like blue ice. "Who was that woman, Michael?"

"Her name is Cookie Hawthorne, and she's an actress. I dated her a couple of times years ago."

"Why did she say your name is Michael Vellini?"

Michael knew he had to make his choice. Now. He could keep lying to Shawn and remain loyal to his father. Or he could tell her the truth.

He met her gaze. He knew the next few minutes

might determine the entire future of their relationship. "Because it is."

"I don't understand."

"DeNiro was my mother's maiden name. My real name is Michael Vellini. My father is Victor Vellini."

"Victor Vellini! But Victor Vellini owns—"

"Yes. He owns The Glass Slipper."

"You're Victor Vellini's son? But why would you pretend to be someone else?"

Michael faced her squarely. "Because someone has been stealing money from the casino. I'm here to try to find out who. And to do that, I had to pretend to be someone else."

The color drained from her face. She clasped her hands together, and Michael could see she was visibly trying to keep her emotions under control.

"You ... So you've been lying to me all along. . . ."

"I'm sorry, Shawn," he continued. "I didn't want to lie to you, but I didn't have a choice."

"Everything ... everything you told me was a lie. . . ." she said slowly. Her face twisted as the import of what he'd told her sank in. "Our lovemaking ... all of it ... a lie!"

"No, that's not true! Not about the lovemaking. That was real. Not about you and me. That's very real. In fact, it's the most real thing in my life."

Her head was shaking from side to side. "All this time. Lies. All of it lies."

"Shawn, please. Think. By the time I got to know you, I was already committed to my story. I couldn't tell you the truth. Please try to understand."

"Understand? I don't understand anything. I . . . I

don't know you at all, Michael. The man I thought I knew doesn't exist.''

''I've never lied to you about anything except my name and the real reason I was in Las Vegas.''

''How can I believe you? How can I believe *anything* you told me? Why, you *still* wouldn't have told me the truth if that actress hadn't come into the casino, would you?''

Deep regret filled Michael. ''No, probably not.''

She stared at him. Slowly, understanding filled her eyes. In an anguished voice she said, ''You deliberately went after me, didn't you? Why? Am I a suspect in your investigation?''

He had hurt her enough. The time for evasion was past. If Michael ever hoped to win Shawn's forgiveness, he needed to tell her everything. She deserved that much.

''You were at one time. You no longer are.''

''I see.'' She looked at him, her eyes filled with some nameless emotion. ''So who *are* your suspects?''

''Shawn, I can't tell—''

''I think I deserve to know everything, Michael,'' she said coldly.

Oh, hell. His cover was blown. He might as well tell her. He was sick of all the subterfuge, anyway. ''Right now the primary suspects are the pit bosses.''

''The pit bosses,'' she repeated slowly. Suddenly the color drained from her face. ''Including my uncle?'' she whispered.

''Yes.'' *Especially your uncle.*

There was an agonizing moment of silence as she processed the information. Michael could almost feel the gears turning in her head. ''He's your primary suspect, isn't he?''

Michael nodded.

"And he was *always* a suspect, wasn't he?"

He nodded again.

"That's the *real* reason you went after me, isn't it, Michael?"

Knowing he was nailing his coffin shut, Michael said, "Yes. But that all changed, Shawn, after I got to know you."

Her face twisted. "Oh, really? You expect me to believe that? You used me, Michael."

"I know it seems that way, but—"

"What other way *could* it seem?" she said, her eyes glinting with anger. She laughed, the sound bitter and not like Shawn at all. "I knew, from the first moment I met you, that there was something odd about your pursuit of me. But did I listen to my instincts? No. I guess I *wanted* to believe you really liked me." She shook her head in disbelief. "What a fool I was. I even thought you . . . Oh, well, what does it matter what I thought? What does any of it matter now?" She turned away from him and looked out the window.

He laid his hand on her arm, feeling the rigidity of it beneath his fingers. "Shawn, please don't say things like that. *You* matter. How we feel about each other matters."

Pulling her arm from his grasp, she whipped her head around and glared at him. "How we *feel* about each other! I'll tell you how I feel about you now, Michael! I despise you! You're a liar and a cheat. And I hope everything you've done comes back to haunt you someday."

It was coming back to haunt him now. Seeing the cold dislike in her eyes was the worst punishment he could have.

"And you're wrong about my uncle, too. I can't wait until you find out just *how* wrong!"

"I hope you're right."

"I know I'm right," she said through gritted teeth. "And I just have one more thing to say to you, Michael Vellini. You can go straight to hell!"

Then, before Michael could stop her, she yanked open the car door and jumped out.

ELEVEN

Shawn cried all the way home. When she finally reached the safety and privacy of her town house, she raced upstairs to her bedroom and threw herself across the bed, where she cried for another hour.

Finally, exhausted, she fell asleep.

She awoke with a pounding headache. She sat up clutching her head. For a minute, she didn't know where she was or why she was there. Then the memories came flooding back.

Michael, she thought. Michael.

Now she remembered everything. She must have fallen asleep. What time was it, anyway? It was dark in the room, and the house was silent. She looked at her bedside clock. Seven o'clock.

She'd been sleeping about an hour.

Rubbing her temples, she got up, walked into the bathroom, and found her bottle of aspirin. After downing two, she splashed her face with cold water, then stared at herself in the mirror.

She looked terrible.

Her hair was a mess. Her face looked blotchy, and her eyes were all red and puffy.

She picked up her comb and tried to work the tangles out of her hair. Finally she just gave up. What did it matter how she looked, anyway?

Slowly, heavily, she walked downstairs. She poured herself a glass of cold water and drank it while staring out the back window. In the milky moonlight, she saw the stark outline of the yucca tree. It looked as lonely and isolated as she felt at that moment.

Everything Michael had said earlier revolved in her mind. Over and over again she replayed their conversation. And each time she did, the pain and shock were like new wounds in a body already battered and bloody.

It was bad enough to find out the truth about Michael and their relationship, but now she had the added problem of what to do next.

She knew what she wanted to do. She wanted to lick her wounds in private. Cut her losses. Get through the pain and desolation somehow and go on with her life.

Should she? Could she? Just forget about all of it, and leave Michael to play his nasty games and spy on people until he found his criminal?

Or should she blow the whistle?

In particular, should she tell her uncle what was going on?

Some part of her didn't want to betray Michael.

The other part of her insisted that Michael didn't deserve her silence or her loyalty.

After all, he had betrayed *her*. God, she had been right about him from the beginning. That first night, the first time she'd seen him, she'd been reminded of her father. And just like Gerald, Michael had betrayed her, too.

She fought against the fresh tears that threatened to spill. She owed Michael nothing. Not now. Why should she have any qualms about exposing him?

Furthermore, if she *didn't* tell her uncle, wouldn't that be a betrayal of her mother? Her family? Didn't her uncle have a right to know he was being investigated?

But what if her uncle really was guilty as Michael had suggested?

Oh, dear God. Please, please don't let him be guilty.

Shawn thought about how much her mother had already suffered at the hands of her father. No woman who had been through all of that deserved to suffer again.

Philip simply *couldn't* be guilty.

Still . . . Shawn remembered how he had paid off that enormous debt of her father's. He'd told her mother that the money came from an inheritance. From an aunt they hadn't even known about.

Had he been lying? Had the money really been embezzled from the casino?

Shawn hugged herself, suddenly chilled.

She'd always thought the story about the aunt was suspect. But she'd thought the money had been Philip's savings and that he hadn't wanted her mother to know because he realized Carolyn would never have allowed him to make that kind of gesture.

But what if Shawn was wrong? What if Philip had stolen the money? What then?

What if Shawn told her uncle about Michael's investigation and Philip was really guilty? Did he deserve this warning? If he was a crook, didn't he deserve to be caught, exposed, and punished?

Please, God. Tell me what to do.

She couldn't come up with an answer that satisfied her.

Finally, not knowing what else to do, she left a note for Annika telling her where she had gone, then she climbed into her car and headed toward her mother's house.

"Shawn! What a nice surprise!" Carolyn said, a welcoming smile on her face. "Come on in. Philip's here. As a matter of fact, we were just talking about you." As usual, she looked great, Shawn thought, dressed in a ruby silk caftan that flowed around her willowy body.

They hugged, then Shawn allowed herself to be led into the bright living room. Her uncle, who had been sitting on the sofa, stood. He looked relaxed and casual in blue jeans and a flannel shirt. There was a cheerful fire burning in the fireplace, and on the coffee table in front of the sofa was a plate of cheese and crackers and two glasses of wine.

"Hello, Shawn," he said.

"Hi."

"Honey, sit down," her mother said. "Would you like something to drink? A glass of wine or a soft drink?"

Shawn sat in the leather wing chair across from the sofa. "How about some coffee?"

"Is instant okay? I *could* put on a pot."

"Instant's fine."

Within minutes, Shawn had her coffee. She sipped the strong brew slowly, still not sure if she was doing the right thing. She eyed her mother over the rim of her cup, then cut her glance to her uncle, who met her gaze.

"Is something wrong, Shawn?" he said as Carolyn reseated herself.

"Why?" Shawn asked.

He shrugged. "You look . . . I don't know." He turned toward her mother, an expression on his face that plainly said, *help me out, here.*

"You look worried," Carolyn said, leaning forward. Her clear blue gaze swept over Shawn. "And tired."

"Is 'tired' a euphemism for 'a complete wreck'?" Shawn asked drily. "Because if it is, you're right. I *am* a complete wreck right now."

"Why, honey? What's happened?"

"Oh, nothing much," Shawn said bitterly. Suddenly her decision was made. She owed Michael nothing. "Except that the man I've been seeing, the man I've trusted, has turned out to be somebody completely different from the man he pretended to be."

"Michael?" Carolyn said softly.

Her uncle frowned. "Pretended to be?"

"Yes. His real name is Michael Vellini." Shawn watched her uncle's face as what she'd just said sank in. Her mother still looked confused.

"I don't understand," Carolyn said, looking first at Shawn and then at Philip.

Philip met Shawn's gaze. "Is Michael related to Victor Vellini?" he finally asked.

"Yes. Victor Vellini is Michael's father."

"Ahh . . ." Philip said, nodding. "That explains some things."

"Yes, doesn't it?" Shawn replied.

"*What* things? Will somebody please explain what's going on?" Carolyn said, a note of exasperation in her voice.

Philip turned to her. "You remember . . . Victor Vellini is the new owner of The Glass Slipper."

"Oh, yes, of course." Then Carolyn's eyes widened. "And Michael is his son?"

Shawn nodded.

"But why hide the fact?" she asked.

"Because," Shawn said, "when his father was in the process of buying the casino, his people discovered that someone has been stealing—helping themselves to some of the blackjack revenue—and Michael was sent in as a sort of undercover spy. To catch the crook."

"Spy!" Carolyn said.

Philip said nothing, but his jaw hardened. His hazel eyes looked thoughtful. "I've been told nothing about this." He frowned. "And I'm the head pit boss."

"There's a reason for that, which I'll tell you about in a minute," Shawn said, once more fighting the pain that threatened to overwhelm her. *Hang on to your anger*, she told herself. *That's a healthier emotion right now.*

"I just can't believe this," Carolyn said. "That nice young man. A spy? Are you *sure*?"

"Oh, yes, I'm sure. He told me so himself. Isn't that just wonderful? He was spying on *me*! That's why he started dating me in the first place."

"Oh, honey . . ."

The compassion in her mother's voice was nearly Shawn's undoing. But from somewhere she called on hidden reserves of strength, and she didn't break down.

"You know," Philip said, "I consider myself a pretty damn good judge of character, and I really *like* Michael. I find it hard to believe that's the only reason he's been seeing you."

Shawn nodded bleakly. "He fooled me, too." When

her uncle started to say something else, she held up her hand. "Wait. There's more. Michael said I'm no longer a suspect. But you are."

He didn't act surprised. He just nodded thoughtfully and said, "Yes. When you said what Michael was doing, I figured I probably was."

"Oh, Philip!" Carolyn said. "How can they suspect *you*? Why, you've been one of their most loyal employees. You've worked at the casino for, what? Twenty-two years?"

"Twenty-four," he said softly.

"Anyway," Shawn said, "I thought you needed to know so you can—" She broke off, catching herself just in time. She had been about to say so he could cover himself, if necessary. "I just thought you needed to know."

Philip stood, rubbing his chin. He walked over to the fireplace and stood staring at the fire for a long time. Shawn and her mother gave each other unhappy looks, then both looked away. The minutes ticked away slowly on the mantel clock. The fire hissed and popped, and somewhere outside, a car door slammed and muted voices could be heard.

Finally Philip heaved a sigh and turned. "I think I'd better go talk with Michael . . . and Dominic Cassione."

Shawn met her mother's gaze. In Carolyn's eyes was reflected the same emotion Shawn now felt.

Fear.

After Shawn left his car so abruptly, Michael considered going after her. Then he decided it might be better to give her some time to cool off. So he went back into the casino and headed for his godfather's office.

"Mr. Cassione left early today," his secretary said. She pushed her glasses up on her nose, reminding Michael of Shawn and causing a sudden ache in the vicinity of his heart.

"Okay. I'll—" He had been about to say he'd try Dominic's suite, and just caught himself in time. "Would you tell him I stopped by? Michael DeNiro."

The secretary nodded, and Michael left. He headed straight for the penthouse but realized when he was halfway there, he didn't have the key for the private elevator with him.

"Dammit," he said.

Back in the lobby of the casino, he found a house phone and punched in the number of Dominic's private line.

There was no answer.

"Double damn!" he muttered. He guessed he might as well go home. Maybe he'd have better luck calling his father.

When he entered the town house complex, he drove by Shawn's unit first. It was dark except for a faint light showing from the small kitchen window.

Was she at home? Was she sitting there in the dark because she didn't want him to know she was there?

Feeling as if the weight of the world were on his shoulders—a weight that was about half guilt and half fear, a fear that nothing he did or said from now on would make one bit of difference to Shawn, that she'd hate him forever—Michael headed for his own unit.

The first thing he did when he got inside was fix himself a hefty scotch on the rocks.

The second thing he did was head for the telephone.

Yolanda answered the phone at his father's. "Your father, he is out," she said.

"When will he be back?"

"I don't know. Maybe eight. Maybe nine. He went to dinner with Mr. Morelli."

"Well, would you please tell him to call me the minute he gets home?" Michael said.

He tried his godfather again.

Still no answer.

Frustrated and miserable, Michael sank onto the couch and gulped down his scotch.

It didn't make him feel any better.

He couldn't rid himself of the picture of Shawn in his car when she'd realized what he was telling her. Her beautiful, soft blue eyes were like chips of ice. Her sweet mouth looked strained and hard. Her face had been white and shocked.

Her anger, although real, had covered a deeper emotion, Michael knew. The emotion was pain: stark and deep and agonizing.

She'd been devastated by his betrayal.

He had known how really vulnerable she was.

Still he'd hurt her.

He'd hurt her in ways no woman should ever be hurt.

And he hated himself for it.

The phone rang at nine-thirty.

"Michael? Yolanda said you called."

"Hi, Dad." Michael picked up his glass of scotch and drained it. His head was pounding. No damn wonder, he thought. He'd lost count of the number of scotches he'd consumed tonight.

"Is something wrong?" Victor asked.

His father was pretty damned perceptive. Michael would give him that. "Yes, something's very definitely wrong." Michael enunciated his words carefully.

"Have you been drinking?" Victor said, his voice hardening.

"Hell, yes, I've been drinking. It isn't every day the woman you love tells you she despises you. I think I deserve to drink!"

"Michael, you're not making any sense."

"What part of what I said don't you understand, Dad?" Michael knew he was being unreasonable as well as rude and disrespectful, but he couldn't seem to help himself.

When Victor spoke, his voice was cold. "Explain yourself, Michael."

Michael rubbed his temple. "Oh, hell, it's simple enough. I've fallen in love with Shawn MacInnes, and today she learned who I *really* am."

"I see," Victor said quietly. "So your cover is blown."

"It is with Shawn." *And she's the only one I care about right now.*

"How did the MacInnes woman—"

"Dad, stop calling Shawn, 'the MacInnes woman.' "

In a very patient voice, his father said, "All right, fine. How did *Shawn* find out who you are, Michael? Did you tell her?"

"Yes, I told her. But I had no choice. Remember Cookie Hawthorne?" When his father didn't say anything, Michael said, "You know, that actress I dated when you first bought into Saturn Studios?"

"Oh. Yes, I think I remember her. What about her?"

"Well, she came into the casino today and recognized me."

His father sighed. "I guess sooner or later something like this was inevitable. The question is, what now?

Do you think the girl . . . Shawn . . . will say anything to anyone else? Her uncle, maybe?"

"I don't know." He squeezed his eyes shut. The top of his head felt as if someone were hitting it with a hammer. "And frankly, right now I really don't care."

"You don't care! You'd better care, Michael. It's your job to care. That's what I pay you to do, and you'd better remember that. In fact, you'd better get your backside over there and talk to that woman. You'd better make damned sure she keeps her mouth shut. Tell her she'll lose her job if she says anything. Do anything you have to do, just keep her quiet!"

Suddenly Michael had had enough. "Oh, I plan to go see her, Dad," he said tightly. "You can rest assured of that. But not because it's my job, because I don't really give a damn about my job anymore. In fact, I quit! No, I'm going over there as soon as we hang up, and maybe, just maybe, if I'm damned lucky, she'll find it in her heart to forgive me!"

When Shawn pulled into her driveway, the sweep of her headlights illuminated Michael leaning against the garage door.

Her heart began to beat wildly.

What was he doing standing there in the dark?

Trying to calm her chaotic emotions, she aimed her control at the door, and as it began to slide up, she told herself to be calm. She refused to look in his direction, but out of the corner of her eye, she saw him walk around behind her car. Ignoring him, she pulled into the garage and shut off her ignition. For a moment she didn't move. Then, telling herself not to be a coward, she took a deep breath, opened her door, and climbed out of the car.

He was standing a few feet away. She stared at him. "What are you doing here?"

"Waiting for you."

"Well, I hope you didn't wait too long, because you've wasted your time. I don't want to talk to you." She turned her back on him and began to walk around the front of the car. She was heading for the door leading into the house.

A second later, he had covered the distance between them and grabbed her arm.

She stopped. "Let go of me." She was proud of herself for sounding so calm and controlled, even though her insides were jumping around like Mexican jumping beans.

"I have to talk to you, Shawn. You've got to listen to me!"

"I said, let go of me!"

He dropped his hand.

She began to walk toward the door again. All she wanted was to get inside before she broke down in front of him.

"I love you, Shawn. I know I wasn't truthful with you, but I've admitted it. Can't you forgive me? Can't you try to understand I was between a rock and a hard place?"

Something hot and very painful pressed itself against her chest and up into her throat. Tears burned in her eyes, and it took all the self-control she possessed not to give in to them. Very slowly, she turned to face him. At that moment, the automatic overhead light went out and the garage was plunged into murky darkness. "You don't know the meaning of love, Michael."

"I know you're angry and hurt, Shawn, and I don't blame you. I deserve whatever you want to dish out."

As he talked, he walked closer until he was so close, she could smell his cologne and see his eyes gleaming. "In your shoes, I'd feel the same way. But please don't throw away what we've shared just because you're hurt. You must believe me, because I do love you. And I never wanted to hurt you. So many times I wanted to tell you who I really was, but I couldn't. You'll never know how sorry I am. How much I wish I could turn back the clock."

"You forgot. There aren't any clocks in Las Vegas." But even as she said the sarcastic words, she wanted to believe him. He sounded so sincere. So genuinely contrite. If only she knew what was true and what wasn't. But how could she? "I'll tell you what I do believe," she said coldly. "I believe you'd say or do anything to get me to do what you want me to do."

She could feel him stiffen. "And what would that be?" he said, his voice soft.

"I'd have to be an imbecile not to figure it out, you know," she continued. "You're worried I might blow your cover. Mouth off at the casino. Tell everyone who you are and what you're *really* doing there. Well, it's too late, Michael, because I've already told my uncle. So you can stop the pretense. You don't need to sweet-talk me any longer."

"Believe it or not, I don't really care that you told your uncle. All I care about right now is you."

"I said you can quit pretending!" she cried.

"Goddammit, I'm *not* pretending! Does this seem like I'm pretending?" And with that, he reached for her, yanking her into his arms. A second later, his mouth clamped down against hers in a bone-jarring kiss that knocked the breath out of her. Shawn tried to push him away, but the more she pushed, the harder he held her, and finally she stopped struggling.

The moment she stopped struggling, the kiss changed. Michael still held her fast, but he no longer kissed her as if he wanted to punish her. Instead, his tongue swept inside her mouth and delved deeply as his hands molded her body to his.

Her heart slammed against her chest, and she could feel his heart hammering equally hard. Soon she was clinging to him and returning his passionate kiss with a wild, desperate passion of her own. As he ground his mouth against hers, she ached with an emptiness that cried to be filled.

They kissed greedily, again and again, and Michael's hands became more insistent as they cupped her bottom and pulled her hard up against him. The heat of him seared her, and an answering heat shot through her. Suddenly nothing mattered except this fire that threatened to consume her.

"Shawn, Shawn," he muttered, his hot mouth trailing down her throat. "I love you. I want you. God, how I want you." His hands moved over her body, sliding up her rib cage to cup her breasts, his thumbs finding the aching nubs.

She moaned, and when she did, the last vestige of his control seemed to vanish. Grunting, he pushed her back against the hood of the car and yanked her blouse out of her skirt with one hand as the other shoved her skirt up. Seconds later, he had the front of her bra unhooked, and his mouth clamped down on one nipple. Shawn cried out.

"Do you want me to stop?" he said, his voice harsh.

She knew she would die if he stopped. "No," she groaned, twisting her head from side to side.

The word was hardly out of her mouth before he reached for her panties and pulled them down. She heard the rasp of a zipper, and then he was driving into her, all heat and steel and a primitive, uncontrollable hunger.

Shawn strained as she met his thrusts. Her fingernails dug into his back as she clutched him tightly. The fire in her was about to rage out of control. Her heart felt as if it might explode.

Suddenly, without warning, an exquisite pleasure that was almost painful shuddered through her. Gasping, she held on to Michael tightly as he continued to thrust. Then, with a mighty heave, she could feel the life force spilling into her, hot and powerful. He cried out, and she clutched him as he gave a great, wracking shudder. Then, spent, he collapsed against her.

Shawn lay there on the hood of her car, her heart still beating like a mad thing. Michael lay against her for a few minutes, then he slowly raised himself up and reached for her.

"Did I hurt you?" he said, his voice ragged.

Shawn wet her lips. "No." Her mind refused to work. She knew that soon she would have to think about what had just happened between them, but she didn't want to think about it now.

"Shawn, look at me," he ordered.

She raised her eyes. There was just enough light to see the gleam in his.

He took her chin in his hand and brought his face close. Then he kissed her. A hard, possessive kiss. When it was over, he said, "I love you. I know you don't believe me, but I intend to prove it to you."

She stared at him. Her body felt as if she'd been swimming a great distance. Her brain felt like mush.

She wanted to say something, but she didn't know what to say. She knew she was in a state of emotional and physical overload.

He pulled her close and smoothed down her hair. "You're exhausted," he said. "Go on in and go to bed now." He set her gently away from him.

She pulled her blouse closed around her. "Michael, I—"

He touched her lips with his fingertips. "Shh, don't say anything."

Sighing, she nodded, then mutely started for the door. By the time she reached it, Michael had walked out to the driveway.

"And Shawn?"

She paused in the act of pushing the button that would lower the garage door.

She looked up.

Michael stood, his lean body a dark silhouette etched against a pool of moonlight just outside the door.

"You belong to me," he said softly. "Don't ever forget that."

TWELVE

You belong to me. Don't ever forget that.

Shawn huddled under the covers. As if she could forget. Her body felt branded.

She couldn't believe she had actually made love with Michael in the garage! On top of her car! With the garage door wide open, where anyone walking by could have seen them!

She squeezed her eyes tightly shut as if she could squeeze out the vivid picture of herself and Michael and their frantic lovemaking.

She lay awake most of the night, and when she finally did fall asleep, her dreams were filled with dark, erotic images. When her alarm went off at six the next morning, she felt as if she'd run a marathon in her sleep.

"My God," Annika exclaimed when, thirty minutes later, Shawn emerged into the hallway. "You look like hell. What's wrong with you?"

"Didn't sleep well," Shawn mumbled, avoiding Annika's eyes.

Later, as Shawn stood at the kitchen counter sipping her coffee, Annika walked in. She frowned. "Hey, are you okay?" Her green eyes were filled with concern.

Shawn shrugged. "I'm all right. No, actually I'm *not* all right. I don't feel well." She set her coffee down. "I think I'm going to call in sick today."

"Good idea." Annika stood there as if she wanted to say something else.

Shawn headed for the wall phone. "Why are you up so early?" she asked as she dialed the number of the casino's personnel office.

"I . . . uh, well, I wanted to talk to you. But make your call first."

Shawn did, then after she hung up, she turned to Annika.

Annika's green eyes shone. "You're never going to believe this, Shawn, but Darryl and I are getting married this weekend."

Shawn's mouth dropped open. "You're kidding! I thought you never wanted to get married!"

Annika grinned sheepishly. "Darryl talked me into it."

"So that means you're moving out. . . ." Oh, God. Just what she needed. Another problem!

"But you don't need to worry," Annika said. "Darryl told me to tell you we'll pay my half of the rent until you find someone else to share this place." Then she grinned. "Hey, you and Michael are getting along so well, maybe he'd—"

"No," Shawn said.

Annika frowned. "What's the matter? Did something happen?"

"I don't want to talk about it."

"Well, okay, but if you ever *do* want to talk, you know I'm always ready to listen."

"I know," Shawn said. "I'm happy for you, Annika. And later I want you to tell me all about it. But right now, if you don't mind, I'm going back to bed. My head is killing me." All Shawn wanted at that moment was to go bury her head under the covers and never come out again.

Of course, she knew she was simply postponing the inevitable. She couldn't stay home forever. She would have to go back to work.

She would have to face Michael again.

She would have to decide whether, this time, he'd been telling her the truth and whether she could forgive him.

But not today.

Michael's phone rang just as he was ready to leave for work. He snatched it up.

"Michael? It's Dominic. Your father called me last night and told me what's happened."

"I knew he would."

"You haven't really quit, have you?"

Michael sighed. "No."

"Good. We must talk this morning."

"Yes, I think so, too."

"I'll send a message down to the pit telling them you're wanted in the Personnel Office. Come straight to my office when you get to work."

"All right."

At eight-ten, when Michael was shown into Dominic's office, he wasn't surprised to see Philip Brownlee there, too. Brownlee stood and shook his hand. "Good morning, Michael."

"Good morning."

"Philip was here waiting when I got to the office, Michael," Dominic explained. "I asked him to join us." He gestured toward his credenza. "There's coffee if you want it."

Michael poured himself a cup, then sat.

"Shawn told me about your investigation," Philip said.

"Yes, I know," Michael answered. "I'm sorry I had to deceive you, sir."

"I understand."

"I wish Shawn did," Michael said.

"Give her some time. She will." Philip fingered some papers on his lap. "But that's not why I'm here. I'm here to clear my name. I brought in a copy of my aunt's will as well as copies of my bank statements, income tax returns, and investment records. I want both of you to know I'm completely clean. In fact, I'd welcome a full-scale investigation into this problem."

"That's exactly what I was going to recommend," Michael said, turning to his godfather. "Uncle Dominic, what do you think?"

Dominic rubbed his chin, dark eyes thoughtful. "Perhaps that's the only option open to us now. But we'll need to talk to your father about it."

"The sooner, the better," Michael said. He turned to Philip. "Now let's look at these records you brought."

It didn't take Michael long to figure out that Philip was telling them the truth. Unless he'd hidden stolen money in Swiss bank accounts or something, all his papers checked out. Michael was especially relieved to read his aunt's will and to see the copy of the check representing the proceeds of her estate. A hefty check. More than enough to cover Gerald MacInnes's debts.

Afterwards, Philip gathered up his papers and prepared to leave.

"Wait," Michael said, "I'll walk out with you. There's something personal I'd like to discuss with you."

"Why don't the two of you just talk here?" Dominic suggested. "I've got something I want to do, anyway."

A few minutes later, when they were alone, Philip said, "This is about Shawn, isn't it?"

"Yes. I just wanted you to know that I realize I've hurt her, and I intend to try to make it up to her. Right now she's still angry with me and feeling betrayed, but I hope to change that. I hope eventually she'll forgive me."

"Do you love her?" Philip asked bluntly.

"Yes."

"Good."

Michael felt a quick rush of relief. "So you approve?" He had been afraid Philip wouldn't, not after what had happened.

"Yes, I do." Philip stood and held out his hand. "And I wish you luck."

Michael took his hand. "Thanks. I have a feeling I'm going to need it."

After calling in sick, Shawn went back to bed. She lay there for a long time, but exhaustion finally claimed her, and she fell asleep.

The ringing telephone woke her.

It was her uncle calling.

"I looked for you at work," he said, "but they told me you were sick. I was worried."

She considered fudging a bit, then decided she wasn't that much of a coward. "Just heartsick, that's all. No need to worry." She rubbed her grainy eyes, "I'm all right now, though. What's going on?"

"I had a long talk with Dominic Cassione and Michael today."

Her heart stopped beating. She was suddenly wide-awake. "Oh? And?"

"And I'd like to talk to you. Can I come over?"

"Yes, but give me an hour, okay?"

"Certainly."

An hour and fifteen minutes later they were seated at the kitchen table over glasses of iced tea.

"What happened, Uncle Philip?"

"I went to Cassione's office first thing this morning. A few minutes later, Michael arrived, and the three of us talked." He traced the condensation on his glass as he spoke. "I decided the best approach was the direct one, so I took all my bank and investment records, my income tax returns, and a copy of Aunt Lydia's will with me."

Shawn expelled a deep breath.

He gave her a quizzical look. "What's the matter?"

"Oh, nothing. I . . . I guess I'm glad you could prove there really *was* an inheritance."

His frown deepened. "You mean you doubted it?"

Shawn smiled sheepishly. "I'm sorry, Uncle Philip. It's just that, well, I'd never even heard of your Aunt Lydia until you paid off my father's debts."

He looked incredulous. "Where did you *think* I'd gotten the money?"

"I thought it came from your savings . . . that you just didn't want Mom to know, so you made up that story about Aunt Lydia dying and leaving you her money."

Philip nodded. "I have to be honest and say I thought

about doing that, but then I got that windfall, and by rights your father should have shared it with me, so I was able to do what I wanted to do without your mother being embarrassed over it." He smiled. "Your mother's feelings are important to me."

"I know they are," Shawn said softly, and for the first time since her mother had told her she and Philip were engaged, Shawn felt no reservations, no faint envy. She got up, came around the table, and hugged her uncle. "Thank you for being so good to my mother. I'm very glad she has you."

He returned her hug.

Shawn sat down again. "I'm also glad you were able to clear your name with the casino."

"Me, too. But that's not why I came over here, Shawn. There's something else I wanted to talk to you about."

"What?"

"Michael."

Shawn looked away. "I'm not sure I want to talk about him."

"You know, Shawn, when you first told me about Michael, I was angry with him. I resented the fact that I was a suspect and that Michael was working at the casino under false pretenses. I especially didn't like that he'd lied to you. But now that I've had a chance to think about all of it, I realize both Michael and his father had a perfect right to do whatever was necessary to find out who's stealing from the casino."

"I can't believe you think what Michael did is all right."

"Shawn, you're not looking at the situation logically. You're too close to it, too emotional."

"Maybe I am, but I can't help it. He betrayed me,

Uncle Philip. He pretended to be someone he's not . . . just like my father did.''

"Shawn, the two situations are not at all similar.''

"I think they're very similar," she said bitterly. She had counted on her father, trusted him, believed in him, and he had let her down. She had counted on Michael, trusted him, believed in him, and he had also let her down.

"I know you loved your father. I loved him, too. But he was a weak man, and he ran out on his responsibilities. He deserted you. Michael hasn't done that. Michael made one mistake, and he's admitted it. He's very sorry he hurt you, and he loves you. Can't you forgive him?''

"I don't know," she cried. "I just don't know." Tears stung her eyes, and she didn't want to cry again.

Her uncle sighed. "Well, honey, all I can say is, don't take too long to think about it. Hanging on to your anger can end up being very lonely.''

When Michael returned to the floor after talking with Shawn's uncle, Jimmy Penner gave him an odd look. "Mr. Cassione sent a message saying he wants to see you again. What's going on, Michael?''

"It's personal," Michael said.

"I didn't know you knew Mr. Cassione," Jimmy persisted.

"He's a friend of my father's." Ignoring Jimmy's continuing curiosity, Michael looked around for Shawn. He didn't see her anywhere. "Is Shawn on her break?''

"She called in sick today," Jimmy said.

"Oh." He wondered if she was really sick or just avoiding him. "Well, I'd better go see what Mr. Cassione wants." As he left the pit again, he saw Luis frowning at him. The natives were getting suspicious, he thought. He wondered if his effectiveness was at an end.

When he reached Dominic's office, Albert, the head security guard, was there. Dominic had a triumphant look on his face. He was holding a videotape in his hand. "We've got our crooks," he said without preamble. "This is yesterday's tape. Wait'll you see it."

Ten minutes later Michael watched as Jimmy Penner, a security guard named Homer Gorski, and a cashier named Slim Shriver helped themselves to several thousand dollars of the previous day's take. It was all there on the tape. They even talked about how much they were taking, so there could be no misunderstandings.

Michael smiled in relief. It was over. The tape could be taken to the prosecutor's office, and the guilty parties would be arrested. As soon as that happened, he could stop pretending to be Michael DeNiro and go back to being Michael Vellini.

"This is great, isn't it?" his godfather said.

Michael went back to the floor and worked the rest of the day. He wished it weren't necessary to keep up his pretense, but he kept telling himself it would only be another day or so.

He wondered how Shawn would feel now. He thought about calling her but decided it might be best to give her another day or so to think about things.

And then, if he had to, he'd camp out on her doorstep until she forgave him.

On Thursday Shawn called in sick again. She knew she'd have to go back to work Friday morning. She couldn't keep hiding forever, much as she might like to.

On Thursday night, Liz stopped by on her way home from work. "Shawn, you're not going to believe this," she said as Shawn let her in, "but Jimmy and Homer Gorski and Slim, the head cashier, were arrested today!"

Shawn stared at her. "Why?" she asked, even though she was sure she knew why.

"For stealing from the casino!" Liz looked shaken. "You know, I was beginning to wonder where Jimmy got all his money, but I had no idea he was *stealing*."

Shawn wasn't sure how she felt about Liz's news. She guessed she was glad the crooks had been caught, but she felt sorry for Liz, who must be feeling just as betrayed as Shawn felt. "Are you doing okay?" she asked.

Liz nodded. "I'm shocked, and I feel pretty stupid for being taken in by Jimmy, but otherwise, I'm doing fine." She grimaced. "It's not like I was in *love* with him or anything."

"Was . . . was Michael there when the arrests were made?" Shawn asked.

Liz gave her a strange look. "Sure. We were all there. Why? What's Michael have to do with this?"

"Nothing." Shawn decided she didn't want to be the one to tell Liz who Michael really was. Liz would be sure to pity her, and Shawn didn't think she could face anyone's pity right now.

"Well, why'd you ask then?"

Shawn shrugged. "I just wondered. I haven't seen him in a couple of days. We . . . uh . . . we had a fight."

Liz nodded sagely. "Yeah, I know how that can be." Then she grinned. "But making up is always nice." Then she said, "But, hey, listen, how're you feeling? What's been wrong with you?"

"Oh, you know, cramps."

"Yeah. Cramps are the pits. So you coming back to work tomorrow?"

"Probably."

After Liz left, Shawn wondered if she'd hear from Michael that night. She hoped not. She wasn't ready to talk to him yet.

When she worked days, she always jogged at night, but she even skipped her run because she didn't want to take a chance on seeing him.

He didn't call.

Friday morning, when Shawn reported for work, the entire casino was buzzing with gossip.

"Boy, Shawn, you sure missed the excitement yesterday," said one of the other blackjack dealers.

"I heard about it."

"Well, I suppose you knew all the time that Michael was really Victor Vellini's son, didn't you?"

Shawn shrugged. She couldn't bring herself to lie, but she also couldn't stand having everyone know how she'd been duped. Her earlier hurt and anger returned as she realized everyone knew she and Michael had been seeing each other.

Well, what did you think? That these people are stupid? You certainly made no secret of the way you felt about him. It was probably written all over your face.

All day long the place seethed with rumors. Information flew back and forth. Shawn tried not to listen or take part, but it was nearly impossible. All around her she heard snatches of conversation.

"I always *knew* there was something fishy about

Jimmy Penner. I mean, he sure did throw money around!''

"And they say Victor Vellini is so rich, he's lost track of how much money he has."

"God," one dealer was heard to say, "imagine being as good-looking as Michael and having all that money, too!"

"I hear he's known as his father's hatchet man," said another.

That was certainly true, Shawn thought miserably. He was also the disappearing man, for she'd not set eyes on him since he left her on Tuesday night.

Just thinking about Tuesday night made her squirm with embarrassment. Of all the stupid things she'd done since meeting Michael, making love in her garage on Tuesday night was the worst. She could excuse her besotted behavior before Tuesday. After all, she hadn't known who and what Michael was then. She'd trusted him.

But Tuesday's actions were totally inexcusable and indefensible.

She'd been like an animal in heat.

She couldn't understand herself. The only thing she could think was that she had temporarily gone crazy.

But she wasn't crazy now.

And the sad, hard fact was that Michael had stayed away from her since that night. Which could only mean one thing: He was regretting his actions and the things he'd said in the heat of the moment, too.

He didn't really love her.

He hadn't meant it when he'd said she belonged to him.

He probably no longer cared whether she forgave him or not.

On and on her thoughts whirled.

The other dealers gave her surreptitious looks throughout the day. Shawn knew they were talking about her, speculating about her and Michael. She refused to acknowledge their looks. She even avoided the lounge when she went on her breaks, walking outside the casino instead.

She thought the day would never be over.

Finally it was.

That night, despite all the things she'd told herself, every time the phone rang, she jumped.

It was never Michael.

Once, not able to help herself, she walked outside just to see if there were lights on in his unit.

There weren't.

The following day was worse. Dozens more stories had surfaced, and the gossip was thicker than ever.

When Shawn went to lunch, she once more avoided the employee lounge. She walked down the street to a little Chinese restaurant she liked. Unfortunately, three other co-workers had the same idea, and short of being rude, and causing even more gossip, she couldn't avoid joining them at their table.

All three were clerks who worked in the cashier's office, and none of them knew that Shawn had been dating Michael, so the situation wasn't as bad as it could have been.

The first woman, whose name was Margie, said, "You worked with Michael Vellini, didn't you, Shawn?"

"Yes." She stood. "I'm kind of in a hurry. I think I'll go hit the buffet right now." Maybe by the time she returned to the table, they'd be talking about something else.

But they followed her to the buffet, and the second woman, whose name was Norma, said, "Did you know Michael Vellini well, Shawn?'

I thought I did. "Yes, I guess so." She piled moo goo gai pan on her plate and moved on.

"I talked to him a couple of times when he came to the office," the third woman, named Gerri, said. "He certainly was a charmer."

Oh, yes, he's a charmer, all right. I can't disagree with that. Shawn took a spoonful of shredded pork and vegetables, then headed toward their table.

When all four of them were settled and eating, Norma said, "It's a shame he's not staying in Las Vegas."

Shawn's heart lurched, and she nearly choked on her forkful of food. "What do you mean?" she finally managed to say.

Margie finished chewing her egg roll, then answered, "I was upstairs earlier this morning, and Mr. Cassione's secretary told me Michael had already gone back to New York. He left yesterday afternoon."

Shawn's appetite disappeared. Michael had gone back to New York. Yesterday. Last night, when she'd been wondering if he'd call her, he was already gone.

And he had gone without telling her.

Which meant she had probably been right in thinking he had had second thoughts about what happened between them.

Somehow she got through the rest of the lunch. Somehow she got through the rest of the afternoon. But as soon as her shift was over, she told Floyd Hazlett, who had been promoted to the position of pit boss, that she wanted to take a few of her vacation days.

"Gee, Shawn, we're really a little shorthanded right now," Floyd said, his big, open face troubled.

"I'm sorry, Floyd, but I've got some personal things going on, and I have to get away for a while."

Somehow she held herself together until she got into her car and starting driving home. Then she let the tears come. She cried and cried. After all the crying she'd done earlier in the week, she was surprised there were any tears left.

But there were. Lots of them.

When she arrived home, she was grateful to see Annika's little Geo gone from her parking slot. Thank God. Shawn knew she couldn't face anyone just now. Annika and Darryl must have already left. They were driving to Lake Tahoe today, where they would be married and spend a few days.

Hurrying inside, Shawn tried to ignore the terrible pain around her heart and the aching sense of loss. She threw herself down on her bed and flung her arm over her eyes.

Michael is gone. Michael is gone. That was her only thought. She tried to keep her mind blank, but memories of the past weeks kept intruding.

She remembered all the days and nights she'd spent with Michael. All the things they'd done and talked about. All the times they'd made love.

In desperation she got up, changed into faded warm-ups, and headed for the loft.

Two hours later, she laid her brush down. It was no good. She wasn't going to get any painting done tonight. She slowly walked downstairs. It was dark outside, she noticed. She thought about making herself something to eat, but the very idea nauseated her.

Suddenly she reversed her direction and went back upstairs. She stripped off her clothes, opened her bedroom window, and climbed into bed.

Michael is gone.

She began to try to picture what her life would be like without him. She told herself she'd be just fine. Maybe she'd quit her job earlier than she'd expected to, perhaps right after Christmas. She could go up to the East Coast and get started on her year-long sabbatical. That would be just the thing to take her mind off Michael.

She knew she was kidding herself.

Oh, she could quit her job and go east as planned. But she wouldn't forget about Michael. She wasn't even sure she could paint if she was this miserable.

Through her uncovered window she saw the moon shining down and the wink of stars far above.

Long after midnight, she fell into a troubled sleep.

The next morning she forced herself to get up. She didn't feel rested. In fact, she felt as if she had a huge, heavy ball pressed right into the middle of her chest. She knew she should go out and run, but she didn't feel like it. Instead she showered, made herself eat some toast, and drank three cups of coffee.

Then, determined, she walked upstairs to the loft. She stared at her painting in progress—a picture done from memory—of a class of young ballet students.

It was garbage.

She ripped it off her drawing table and taped down a blank piece of watercolor paper.

Fighting tears, she went into her bedroom and unearthed her photo album. She flipped through the pages until she found the photo she wanted. Then, slowly, she carried it back to the loft.

She began to sketch.

Hours later, as she layered paint over her initial wash, her picture began to shake shape. With each brushstroke, the tight ball in her chest loosened a bit, and then a bit more.

About four o'clock that afternoon, she finished. She stood back and looked at her painting.

Her father's face looked back at her.

And for the first time since he'd killed himself, Shawn wasn't angry with him.

Her uncle had been right. Her father had been weak. But that hadn't meant that he didn't love her or her mother. He hadn't meant to betray them. He simply hadn't been strong enough to face his problems. Instead, he'd gone away.

Shawn stared at the picture a long time. Tears ran down her face. *I forgive you, Daddy.*

And as she said the words to herself, she knew she could forgive Michael, too.

Michael had done what he had to do. In his place, she would probably have done the same thing.

But, oh, God, she was going to miss him.

How she would miss him.

Worn-out from her emotional day, she started downstairs. She was beginning to feel hungry. As she reached the bottom step, the doorbell rang.

She didn't want to see anyone. She froze on the bottom step. If she didn't answer the door, whoever it was would go away eventually.

The doorbell rang again.

She didn't move.

Now her visitor pounded on the front door. Shawn frowned in irritation. Who in the world was it? And why didn't they just leave? Wasn't it obvious no one was home?

"Shawn?" The pounding continued. "Shawn! It's Michael."

Her heart slammed into her chest. "Michael," she whispered. Like a sleepwalker, she walked toward the door.

"Shawn! Open the door! It's Michael." He rattled the doorknob.

She unlocked the dead bolt and pulled the door open.

He stood there for a minute, just staring at her. It was the longest minute of her life. Her dazed mind could hardly believe he was there. She took in his jeans, his leather boots, the white cable-knit sweater he wore, the way the afternoon sunlight dappled his dark hair, and the expression in his eyes.

Then he smiled, and something inside Shawn fell apart. He stepped inside and shut the door behind him, then he opened his arms, and she flew into them.

When his mouth took hers, she twined her arms around him as if she'd never let him go. A long time later, they finally surfaced for air.

He held her head close to his chest. "God, Shawn, I've missed you the past couple of days," he said.

Shawn smiled tremulously. "I thought you'd gone for good." Her heart was singing. Michael was here.

Tipping her chin up, he gazed down into her eyes. "Without you? Never. I love you, Shawn. Do you believe that now?"

"Yes," she whispered, because she did. She did. She could see the love shining in his eyes.

"Have you forgiven me?"

"Yes. I've forgiven you."

He held her close again, and she could hear his heart beating. "Shawn, how could you think I'd left, for good?" He sounded incredulous. "Especially after Tuesday night. Didn't I tell you you belonged to me?"

"I thought . . . Oh, it doesn't matter what I thought."

"Let's go sit in the living room," he said. "I've got something to show you. Then you'll understand why I went to New York."

When they were seated side by side on the couch, he reached inside the pocket of his jeans and pulled out a small jeweler's box. He handed it to her. "Open it," he said softly.

Shawn's fingers trembled as she held the box and noticed that the velvet was a little worn-looking. Then, slowly, she opened it. Inside was a lovely, old-fashioned ring in the shape of a heart. The center stone was a large diamond, and tiny pavé diamonds bordered it.

"It was my mother's," Michael said softly. "I kept it in the safe in my apartment, and I didn't want to ask you to marry me without it."

Shawn couldn't speak. Her throat was clogged with tears.

Michael took the ring out of the box and slipped it on her ring finger. "You *will* marry me, won't you, Shawn?"

"Oh, Michael! You know I will."

"Well, will you please tell me you love me, then?"

"Of course I love you!" Then she realized that she'd never said so. She threw her arms around him. "Oh, Michael, I love you so much. You can't imagine how much. And I want to marry you more than anything in the world.''

''Then *why* are you crying?''

Shawn started to laugh. She hadn't even realized she was crying, but now she could feel the tears on her cheeks. ''I'm crying because I'm so happy!''

Just before Michael's lips met hers again, he chuckled and said, ''And to think I thought I understood women!''

EPILOGUE

From the society pages of the *New York Times:*

St. Patrick's Cathedral was the setting Saturday for the magnificent wedding of Michael Victor Vellini, son of Victor Vellini, one of New York's most successful movers and shakers, and the late Rosalie Vellini. His bride is the lovely artist Shawn Carolyn MacInnes, whom he met last fall in Las Vegas while working in his father's casino, The Glass Slipper.

The bride looked beautiful in a lace gown designed especially for her by up-and-coming designer Alaina Heatherton. She carried flowers from Royer's and wore pearls by Amanni.

The wedding reception was held upstairs at The Russian Tea Room.

After a wedding trip to Italy, the newlyweds will make their home in the Saratoga area, where the *groom has recently opened a restaurant. Knowing the Vellini touch, Michael's will soon be the most popular restaurant in the area.*

SHARE THE FUN . . .
SHARE YOUR NEW-FOUND TREASURE!!

You don't want to let your new books out of your sight?
That's okay. Your friends can get their own. Order below.